Nomads of the North

Nomads of the North

A Story of Romance and Adventure Under the Open Stars

James Oliver Curwood

MINT EDITIONS

Nomads of the North: A Story of Romance and Adventure Under the Open Stars was first published in 1919.

This edition published by Mint Editions 2021.

ISBN 9781513280707 | E-ISBN 9781513285726

Published by Mint Editions®

 MINT
EDITIONS

minteditionbooks.com

Publishing Director: Jennifer Newens
Design & Production: Rachel Lopez Metzger
Project Manager: Micaela Clark
Typesetting: Westchester Publishing Services

Contents

I

It was late in the month of March, at the dying-out of the Eagle Moon, that Neewa the black bear cub got his first real look at the world. Noozak, his mother, was an old bear, and like an old person she was filled with rheumatics and the desire to sleep late. So instead of taking a short and ordinary nap of three months this particular winter of little Neewa's birth she slept four, which, made Neewa, who was born while his mother was sound asleep, a little over two months old instead of six weeks when they came out of den.

In choosing this den Noozak had gone to a cavern at the crest of a high, barren ridge, and from this point Neewa first looked down into the valley. For a time, coming out of darkness into sunlight, he was blinded. He could hear and smell and feel many things before he could see. And Noozak, as though puzzled at finding warmth and sunshine in place of cold and darkness, stood for many minutes sniffing the wind and looking down upon her domain.

For two weeks an early spring had been working its miracle of change in that wonderful country of the northland between Jackson's Knee and the Shamattawa River, and from north to south between God's Lake and the Churchill.

It was a splendid world. From the tall pinnacle of rock on which they stood it looked like a great sea of sunlight, with only here and there patches of white snow where the winter winds had piled it deep. Their ridge rose up out of a great valley. On all sides of them, as far as a man's eye could have reached, there were blue and black patches of forest, the shimmer of lakes still partly frozen, the sunlit sparkle of rivulet and stream, and the greening open spaces out of which rose the perfumes of the earth. These smells drifted up like tonic and food to the nostrils of Noozak the big bear. Down there the earth was already swelling with life. The buds on the poplars were growing fat and near the bursting point; the grasses were sending out shoots tender and sweet; the camas were filling with juice; the shooting stars, the dog-tooth violets, and the spring beauties were thrusting themselves up into the warm glow of the sun, inviting Noozak and Neewa to the feast. All these things Noozak smelled with the experience and the knowledge of twenty years of life behind her—the delicious aroma of the spruce and the jackpine; the dank, sweet scent of water-lily roots and swelling bulbs that came from a thawed-out fen at the foot of the ridge; and over all these things, overwhelming their individual sweetnesses in a still greater thrill of life, the smell of the heart itself!

And Neewa smelled them. His amazed little body trembled and thrilled for the first time with the excitement of life. A moment before in darkness, he found himself now in a wonderland of which he had never so much as had a dream. In these few minutes Nature was at work upon him. He possessed no knowledge, but instinct was born within him. He knew this was His world, that the sun and the warmth were for him, and that the sweet things of the earth were inviting him into his heritage. He puckered up his little brown nose and sniffed the air, and the pungency of everything that was sweet and to be yearned for came to him.

And he listened. His pointed ears were pricked forward, and up to him came the drone of a wakening earth. Even the roots of the grasses must have been singing in their joy, for all through that sunlit valley there was the low and murmuring music of a country that was at peace because it was empty of men. Everywhere was the rippling sound of running water, and he heard strange sounds that he knew was life; the twittering of a rock-sparrow, the silver-toned aria of a black-throated thrush down in the fen, the shrill paean of a gorgeously coloured Canada jay exploring for a nesting place in a brake of velvety balsam. And then, far over his head, a screaming cry that made him shiver. It was instinct again that told him in that cry was danger. Noozak looked up, and saw the shadow of Upisk, the great eagle, as it flung itself between the sun and the earth. Neewa saw the shadow, and cringed nearer to his mother.

And Noozak—so old that she had lost half her teeth, so old that her bones ached on damp and chilly nights, and her eyesight was growing dim—was still not so old that she did not look down with growing exultation upon what she saw. Her mind was travelling beyond the mere valley in which they had wakened. Off there beyond the walls of forest, beyond the farthest lake, beyond the river and the plain, were the illimitable spaces which gave her home. To her came dully a sound uncaught by Neewa—the almost unintelligible rumble of the great waterfall. It was this, and the murmur of a thousand trickles of running water, and the soft wind breathing down in the balsam and spruce that put the music of spring into the air.

At last Noozak heaved a great breath out of her lungs and with a grunt to Neewa began to lead the way slowly down among the rocks to the foot of the ridge.

In the golden pool of the valley it was even warmer than on the crest of the ridge. Noozak went straight to the edge of the slough. Half a dozen rice birds rose with a whir of wings that made Neewa almost upset himself. Noozak paid no attention to them. A loon let out a squawky protest at Noozak's soft-footed appearance, and followed it up with a raucous screech that raised the hair on Neewa's spine. And Noozak paid no attention to this. Neewa observed these things. His eye was on her, and instinct had already winged his legs with the readiness to run if his mother should give the signal. In his funny little head it was developing very quickly that his mother was a most wonderful creature. She was by all odds the biggest thing alive—that is, the biggest that stood on legs, and moved. He was confident of this for a space of perhaps two minutes, when they came to the end of the fen. And here was a sudden snort, a crashing of bracken, the floundering of a huge body through knee-deep mud, and a monstrous bull moose, four times as big as Noozak, set off in lively flight. Neewa's eyes all but popped from his head. And STILL Noozak PAID No ATTENTION!

It was then that Neewa crinkled up his tiny nose and snarled, just as he had snarled at Noozak's ears and hair and at sticks he had worried in the black cavern. A glorious understanding dawned upon him. He could snarl at anything he wanted to snarl at, no matter how big. For everything ran away from Noozak his mother.

All through this first glorious day Neewa was discovering things, and with each hour it was more and more impressed upon him that his mother was the unchallenged mistress of all this new and sunlit domain.

Noozak was a thoughtful old mother of a bear who had reared fifteen or eighteen families in her time, and she travelled very little this first day in order that Neewa's tender feet might toughen up a bit. They scarcely left the fen, except to go into a nearby clump of trees where Noozak used her claws to shred a spruce that they might get at the juice and slimy substance just under the bark. Neewa liked this dessert after their feast of roots and bulbs, and tried to claw open a tree on his own account. By mid-afternoon Noozak had eaten until her sides bulged out, and Neewa himself—between his mother's milk and the many odds and ends of other things—looked like an over-filled pod. Selecting a spot where the declining sun made a warm oven of a great white rock, lazy old Noozak lay down for a nap, while Neewa, wandering about in quest of an adventure of his own, came face to face with a ferocious bug.

The creature was a giant wood-beetle two inches long. Its two battling pincers were jet black, and curved like hooks of iron. It was a rich brown in colour and in the sunlight its metallic armour shone in a dazzling splendour. Neewa, squatted flat on his belly, eyed it with a swiftly beating heart. The beetle was not more than a foot away, and ADVANCING! That was the curious and rather shocking part of it. It was the first living thing he had met with that day that had not run away. As it advanced slowly on its two rows of legs the beetle made a clicking sound that Neewa heard quite distinctly. With the fighting blood of his father, Soominitik, nerving him on to the adventure he thrust out a hesitating paw, and instantly Chegawasse, the beetle, took upon himself a most ferocious aspect. His wings began humming like a buzz-saw, his pincers opened until they could have taken in a man's finger, and he vibrated on his legs until it looked as though he might be performing some sort of a dance. Neewa jerked his paw back and after a moment or two Chegawasse calmed himself and again began to ADVANCE!

Neewa did not know, of course, that the beetle's field of vision ended about four inches from the end of his nose; the situation, consequently, was appalling. But it was never born in a son of a father like Soominitik to run from a bug, even at nine weeks of age. Desperately he thrust out his paw again, and unfortunately for him one of his tiny claws got a half Nelson on the beetle and held Chegawasse on his shining back so that he could neither buzz not click. A great exultation swept through Neewa. Inch by inch he drew his paw in until the beetle was within reach of his sharp little teeth. Then he smelled of him.

That was Chegawasse's opportunity. The pincers closed and Noozak's slumbers were disturbed by a sudden bawl of agony. When she raised her head Neewa was rolling about as if in a fit. He was scratching and snarling and spitting. Noozak eyed him speculatively for some moments, then reared herself slowly and went to him. With one big paw she rolled him over—and saw Chegawasse firmly and determinedly attached to her offspring's nose. Flattening Neewa on his back so that he could not move she seized the beetle between her teeth, bit slowly until Chegawasse lost his hold, and then swallowed him.

From then until dusk Neewa nursed his sore nose. A little before dark Noozak curled herself up against the big rock, and Neewa took his supper. Then he made himself a nest in the crook of her big, warm forearm. In spite of his smarting nose he was a happy bear, and at the end of his first day he felt very brave and very fearless, though he was but nine weeks old. He had come into the world, he had looked upon many things, and if he had not conquered he at least had gone gloriously through the day.

II

That night Neewa had a hard attack of Mistu-puyew, or stomach-ache. Imagine a nursing baby going direct from its mother's breast to a beefsteak! That was what Neewa had done. Ordinarily he would not have begun nibbling at solid foods for at least another month, but nature seemed deliberately at work in a process of intensive education preparing him for the mighty and unequal struggle which he would have to put up a little later. For hours Neewa moaned and wailed, and Noozak muzzled his bulging little belly with her nose, until finally he vomited and was better.

After that he slept. When he awoke he was startled by opening his eyes full into the glare of a great blaze of fire. Yesterday he had seen the sun, golden and shimmering and far away. But this was the first time he had seen it come up over the edge of the world on a spring morning in the Northland. It was as red as blood, and as he stared it rose steadily and swiftly until the flat side of it rounded out and it was a huge ball of SOMETHING. At first he thought it was Life—some monstrous creature sailing up over the forest toward them—and he turned with a whine of enquiry to his mother. Whatever it was, Noozak was unafraid. Her big head was turned toward it, and she was blinking her eyes in solemn comfort. It was then that Neewa began to feel the pleasing warmth of the red thing, and in spite of his nervousness he began to purr in the glow of it. From red the sun turned swiftly to gold, and the whole valley was transformed once more into a warm and pulsating glory of life.

For two weeks after this first sunrise in Neewa's life Noozak remained near the ridge and the slough. Then came the day, when Neewa was eleven weeks old, that she turned her nose toward the distant black forests and began the summer's peregrination. Neewa's feet had lost their tenderness, and he weighed a good six pounds. This was pretty good considering that he had only weighed twelve ounces at birth.

From the day when Noozak set off on her wandering TREK Neewa's real adventures began. In the dark and mysterious caverns of the forests there were places where the snow still lay unsoftened by the sun, and for two days Neewa yearned and whined for the sunlit valley. They passed the waterfall, where Neewa looked for the first tune on a rushing torrent of water. Deeper and darker and gloomier grew the forest Noozak was

JAMES OLIVER CURWOOD

penetrating. In this forest Neewa received his first lessons in hunting. Noozak was now well in the "bottoms" between the Jackson's Knee and Shamattawa waterway divides, a great hunting ground for bears in the early spring. When awake she was tireless in her quest for food, and was constantly digging in the earth, or turning over stones and tearing rotting logs and stumps into pieces. The little gray wood-mice were her piece de resistance, small as they were, and it amazed Neewa to see how quick his clumsy old mother could be when one of these little creatures was revealed. There were times when Noozak captured a whole family before they could escape. And to these were added frogs and toads, still partly somnambulent; many ants, curled up as if dead, in the heart of rotting logs; and occasional bumble-bees, wasps, and hornets. Now and then Neewa took a nibble at these things. On the third day Noozak uncovered a solid mass of hibernating vinegar ants as large as a man's two fists, and frozen solid. Neewa ate a quantity of these, and the sweet, vinegary flavour of them was delicious to his palate.

As the days progressed, and living things began to crawl out from under logs and rocks, Neewa discovered the thrill and excitement of hunting on his own account. He encountered a second beetle, and killed it. He killed his first wood-mouse. Swiftly there were developing in him the instincts of Soominitik, his scrap-loving old father, who lived three or four valleys to the north of their own, and who never missed an opportunity to get into a fight. At four months of age, which was late in May, Neewa was eating many things that would have killed most cubs of his age, and there wasn't a yellow streak in him from the tip of his saucy little nose to the end of his stubby tail. He weighed nine pounds at this date and was as black as a tar-baby.

It was early in June that the exciting event occurred which brought about the beginning of the big change in Neewa's life, and it was on a day so warm and mellow with sunshine that Noozak started in right after dinner to take her afternoon nap. They were out of the lower timber country now, and were in a valley through which a shallow stream wriggled and twisted around white sand-bars and between pebbly shores. Neewa was sleepless. He had less desire than ever to waste a glorious afternoon in napping. With his little round eyes he looked out on a wonderful world, and found it calling to him. He looked at his mother, and whined. Experience told him that she was dead to the world for hours to come, unless he tickled her foot or nipped her ear, and then she would only rouse herself enough to growl at him. He was tired of that. He yearned for something more exciting, and with his mind suddenly made up he set off in quest of adventure.

In that big world of green and golden colours he was a little black ball nearly as wide as he was long. He went down to the creek, and looked back. He could still see his mother. Then his feet paddled in the soft white sand of a long bar that edged the shore, and he forgot Noozak. He went to the end of the bar, and turned up on the green shore where the young grass was like velvet under his paws. Here he began turning over small stones for ants. He chased a chipmunk that ran a close and furious race with him for twenty seconds. A little later a huge snow-shoe rabbit got up almost under his nose, and he chased that until in a dozen long leaps Wapoos disappeared in a thicket. Neewa wrinkled up his nose and emitted a squeaky snarl. Never had Soominitik's blood run so riotously within him. He wanted to get hold of something. For the first time in his life he was yearning for a scrap. He was like a small boy who the day after Christmas has a pair of boxing gloves and no opponent. He sat down and looked about him querulously, still wrinkling his nose and snarling defiantly. He had the whole world beaten. He knew that. Everything was afraid of his mother. Everything was afraid of Him. It was disgusting—this lack of something alive for an ambitious young fellow to fight. After all, the world was rather tame.

He set off at a new angle, came around the edge of a huge rock, and suddenly stopped.

From behind the other end of the rock protruded a huge hind paw. For a few moments Neewa sat still, eyeing it with a growing anticipation. This time he would give his mother a nip that would waken her for good! He would rouse her to the beauty and the opportunities of this day if there was any rouse in him! So he advanced slowly and cautiously, picked out a nice bare spot on the paw, and sank his little teeth in it to the gums.

There followed a roar that shook the earth. Now it happened that the paw did not belong to Noozak, but was the personal property of Makoos, an old he-bear of unlovely disposition and malevolent temper. But in him age had produced a grouchiness that was not at all like the grandmotherly peculiarities of old Noozak. Makoos was on his feet fairly before Neewa realized that he had made a mistake. He was not only an old bear and a grouchy bear, but he was also a hater of cubs. More than once in his day he had committed the crime of cannibalism. He was what the Indian hunter calls uchan—a bad bear, an eater of his

JAMES OLIVER CURWOOD

own kind, and the instant his enraged eyes caught sight of Neewa he let out another roar.

At that Neewa gathered his fat little legs under his belly and was off like a shot. Never before in his life had he run as he ran now. Instinct told him that at last he had met something which was not afraid of him, and that he was in deadly peril. He made no choice of direction, for now that he had made this mistake he had no idea where he would find his mother. He could hear Makoos coming after him, and as he ran he set up a bawling that was filled with a wild and agonizing prayer for help. That cry reached the faithful old Noozak. In an instant she was on her feet—and just in time. Like a round black ball shot out of a gun Neewa sped past the rock where she had been sleeping, and ten jumps behind him came Makoos. Out of the corner of his eye he saw his mother, but his momentum carried him past her. In that moment Noozak leapt into action. As a football player makes a tackle she rushed out just in time to catch old Makoos with all her weight full broadside in the ribs, and the two old bears rolled over and over in what to Neewa was an exciting and glorious mix-up.

He had stopped, and his eyes bulged out like shining little onions as he took in the scene of battle. He had longed for a fight but what he saw now fairly paralyzed him. The two bears were at it, roaring and tearing each other's hides and throwing up showers of gravel and earth in their deadly clinch. In this first round Noozak had the best of it. She had butted the wind out of Makoos in her first dynamic assault, and now with her dulled and broken teeth at his throat she was lashing him with her sharp hind claws until the blood streamed from the old barbarian's sides and he bellowed like a choking bull. Neewa knew that it was his pursuer who was getting the worst of it, and with a squeaky cry for his mother to lambast the very devil out of Makoos he ran back to the edge of the arena, his nose crinkled and his teeth gleaming in a ferocious snarl. He danced about excitedly a dozen feet from the fighters, Soominitik's blood filling him with a yearning for the fray and yet he was afraid.

Then something happened that suddenly and totally upset the maddening joy of his mother's triumph. Makoos, being a he-bear, was of necessity skilled in fighting, and all at once he freed himself from Noozak's jaws, wallowed her under him, and in turn began ripping the hide off old Noozak's carcass in such quantities that she let out an agonized bawling that turned Neewa's little heart into stone.

It is a matter of most exciting conjecture what a small boy will do when he sees his father getting licked. If there is an axe handy he is liable to use it. The most cataclysmic catastrophe that cam come into his is to have a father whom some other boy's father has given a walloping. Next to being President of the United States the average small boy treasures the desire to possess a parent who can whip any other two-legged creature that wears trousers. And there were a lot of human things about Neewa. The louder his mother bawled the more distinctly he felt the shock of his world falling about him. If Noozak had lost a part of her strength in her old age her voice, at least, was still unimpaired, and such a spasm of outcry as she emitted could have been heard at least half a mile away.

Neewa could stand no more. Blind with rage, he darted in. It was chance that closed his vicious little jaws on a toe that belonged to Makoos, and his teeth sank into the flesh like two rows of ivory needles. Makoos gave a tug, but Neewa held on, and bit deeper. Then Makoos drew up his leg and sent it out like a catapault, and in spite of his determination to hang on Neewa found himself sailing wildly through the air. He landed against a rock twenty feet from the fighters with a force that knocked the wind out of him, and for a matter of eight or ten seconds after that he wobbled dizzily in his efforts to stand up. Then his vision and his senses returned and he gazed on a scene that brought all the blood pounding back into his body again.

Makoos was no longer fighting, but was RUNNING AWAY—and there was a decided limp in his gait!

Poor old Noozak was standing on her feet, facing the retreating enemy. She was panting like a winded calf. Her jaws were agape. Her tongue lolled out, and blood was dripping in little trickles from her body to the ground. She had been thoroughly and efficiently mauled. She was beyond the shadow of a doubt a whipped bear. Yet in that glorious flight of the enemy Neewa saw nothing of Noozak's defeat. Their enemy was RUNNING AWAY! Therefore, he was whipped. And with excited little squeaks of joy Neewa ran to his mother.

III

As they stood in the warm sunshine of this first day of June, watching the last of Makoos as he fled across the creek bottom, Neewa felt very much like an old and seasoned warrior instead of a pot-bellied, round-faced cub of four months who weighed nine pounds and not four hundred.

It was many minutes after Neewa had sunk his ferocious little teeth deep into the tenderest part of the old he-bear's toe before Noozak could get her wind sufficiently to grunt. Her sides were pumping like a pair of bellows, and after Makoos had disappeared beyond the creek Neewa sat down on his chubby bottom, perked his funny ears forward, and eyed his mother with round and glistening eyes that were filled with uneasy speculation. With a wheezing groan Noozak turned and made her way slowly toward the big rock alongside which she had been sleeping when Neewa's fearful cries for help had awakened her. Every bone in her aged body seemed broken or dislocated. She limped and sagged and moaned as she walked, and behind her were left little red trails of blood in the green grass. Makoos had given her a fine pummeling.

She lay down, gave a final groan, and looked at Neewa, as if to say:

"If you hadn't gone off on some deviltry and upset that old viper's temper this wouldn't have happened. And now—look at ME!"

A young bear would have rallied quickly from the effects of the battle, but Noozak lay without moving all the rest of that afternoon, and the night that followed. And that night was by all odds the finest that Neewa had ever seen. Now that the nights were warm, he had come to love the moon even more than the sun, for by birth and instinct he was more a prowler in darkness than a hunter of the day. The moon rose out of the east in a glory of golden fire. The spruce and balsam forests stood out like islands in a yellow sea of light, and the creek shimmered and quivered like a living thing as it wound its way through the glowing valley. But Neewa had learned his lesson, and though the moon and the stars called to him he hung close to his mother, listening to the carnival of night sound that came to him, but never moving away from her side.

With the morning Noozak rose to her feet, and with a grunting command for Neewa to follow she slowly climbed the sun-capped ridge. She was in no mood for travel, but away back in her head was an unexpressed fear that villainous old Makoos might return, and she knew that another fight would do her up entirely, in which event Makoos would make a breakfast of Neewa. So she urged herself down the other side of the ridge, across a new valley, and through a cut that opened like a wide door into a rolling plain that was made up of meadows and lakes and great sweeps of spruce and cedar forest. For a week Noozak had been making for a certain creek in this plain, and now that the presence of Makoos threatened behind she kept at her journeying until Neewa's short, fat legs could scarcely hold up his body.

It was mid-afternoon when they reached the creek, and Neewa was so exhausted that he had difficulty in climbing the spruce up which his mother sent him to take a nap. Finding a comfortable crotch he quickly fell asleep—while Noozak went fishing.

The creek was alive with suckers, trapped in the shallow pools after spawning, and within an hour she had the shore strewn with them. When Neewa came down out of his cradle, just at the edge of dusk, it was to a feast at which Noozak had already stuffed herself until she looked like a barrel. This was his first meal of fish, and for a week thereafter he lived in a paradise of fish. He ate them morning, noon, and night, and when he was too full to eat he rolled in them. And Noozak stuffed herself until it seemed her hide would burst. Wherever they moved they carried with them a fishy smell that grew older day by day, and the older it became the more delicious it was to Neewa and his mother. And Neewa grew like a swelling pod. In that week he gained three pounds. He had given up nursing entirely now, for Noozak— being an old bear—had dried up to a point where she was hopelessly disappointing.

It was early in the evening of the eighth day that Neewa and his mother lay down in the edge of a grassy knoll to sleep after their day's feasting. Noozak was by all odds the happiest old bear in all that part of the northland. Food was no longer a problem for her. In the creek, penned up in the pools, were unlimited quantities of it, and she had encountered no other bear to challenge her possession of it. She looked ahead to uninterrupted bliss in their happy hunting grounds until midsummer storms emptied the pools, or the berries ripened. And Neewa, a happy little gourmand, dreamed with her.

It was this day, just as the sun was setting, that a man on his hands and knees was examining a damp patch of sand five or six miles down the creek. His sleeves were rolled up, baring his brown arms halfway to the shoulders and he wore no hat, so that the evening breeze ruffled a ragged head of blond hair that for a matter of eight or nine months had been cut with a hunting knife.

Close on one side of this individual was a tin pail, and on the other, eying him with the keenest interest, one of the homeliest and yet one of the most companionable-looking dog pups ever born of a Mackenzie hound father and a mother half Airedale and half Spitz.

With this tragedy of blood in his veins nothing in the world could have made the pup anything more than "just dog." His tail,—stretched out straight on the sand, was long and lean, with a knot at every joint; his paws, like an overgrown boy's feet, looked like small boxing-gloves; his head was three sizes too big for his body, and accident had assisted Nature in the perfection of her masterpiece by robbing him of a half of one of his ears. As he watched his master this half of an ear stood up like a galvanized stub, while the other—twice as long—was perked forward in the deepest and most interested enquiry. Head, feet, and tail were Mackenzie hound, but the ears and his lank, skinny body was a battle royal between Spitz and Airedale. At his present inharmonious stage of development he was the doggiest dog-pup outside the alleys of a big city.

For the first time in several minutes his master spoke, and Miki wiggled from stem to stern in appreciation of the fact that it was directly to him the words were uttered.

"It's a mother and a cub, as sure as you're a week old, Miki," he said. "And if I know anything about bears they were here some time to-day!"

He rose to his feet, made note of the deepening shadows in the edge of the timber, and filled his pail with water. For a few moments the last rays of the sun lit up his face. It was a strong, hopeful face. In it was the joy of life. And now it was lighted up with a sudden inspiration, and a glow that was not of the forest alone came into his eyes, as he added:

"Miki, I'm lugging your homely carcass down to the Girl because you're an unpolished gem of good nature and beauty—and for those two things I know she'll love you. She is my sister, you know. Now, if I could only take that cub along with you—"

He began to whistle as he turned with his pail of water in the direction of a thin fringe of balsams a hundred yards away.

Close at his heels followed Miki.

Challoner, who was a newly appointed factor of the Great Hudson's Bay Company, had pitched his camp at tie edge of the lake dose to the mouth of the creek. There was not much to it—a battered tent, a still more battered canoe, and a small pile of dunnage. But in the last glow of the sunset it would have spoken volumes to a man with an eye trained to the wear and the turmoil of the forests. It was the outfit of a man who had gone unfearing to the rough edge of the world. And now what was left of it was returning with him. To Challoner there was something of human comradeship in these remnants of things that had gone through the greater part of a year's fight with him. The canoe was warped and battered and patched; smoke and storm had blackened his tent until it was the colour of rusty char, and his grub sacks were next to empty.

Over a small fire title contents of a pan and a pot were brewing when he returned with Miki at his heels, and close to the heat was a battered and mended reflector in which a bannock of flour and water was beginning to brown. In one of the pots was coffee, in the other a boiling fish.

Miki sat down on his angular haunches so that the odour of the fish filled his nostrils. This, he had discovered, was the next thing to eating. His eyes, as they followed Challoner's final preparatory movements, were as bright as garnets, and every third or fourth breath he licked his chops, and swallowed hungrily. That, in fact, was why Miki had got his name. He was always hungry, and apparently always empty, no matter how much he ate. Therefore his name, Miki, "The drum."

It was not until they had eaten the fish and the bannock, and Challoner had lighted his pipe, that he spoke what was in his mind.

"To-morrow I'm going after that bear," he said.

Miki, curled up near the dying embers, gave his tail a club-like thump in evidence of the fact that he was listening.

"I'm going to pair you up with the cub, and tickle the Girl to death."

Miki thumped his tail harder than before.

"Fine," he seemed to say.

"Just think of it," said Challoner, looking over Miki's head a thousand miles away, "Fourteen months—and at last we're going home. I'm going to train you and the cub for that sister of mine. Eh, won't you like that? You don't know what she's like, you homely little devil, or you wouldn't sit there staring at me like a totem-pole pup! And it isn't in your stupid head to imagine how pretty she is. You saw that sunset to-night? Well, she's prettier than THAT if she is my sister. Got anything to add to that, Miki? If not, let's say our prayers and go to bed!"

JAMES OLIVER CURWOOD

Challoner rose and stretched himself. His muscles cracked. He felt life surging like a giant within him.

And Miki, thumping his tail until this moment, rose on his overgrown legs and followed his master into their shelter.

It was in the gray light of the early summer dawn when Challoner came forth again, and rekindled the fire. Miki followed a few moments later, and his master fastened the end of a worn tent-rope around his neck and tied the rope to a sapling. Another rope of similar length Challoner tied to the corners of a grub sack so that it could be carried over his shoulder like a game bag. With the first rose-flush of the sun he was ready for the trail of Neewa and his mother. Miki set up a melancholy wailing when he found himself left behind, and when Challoner looked back the pup was tugging and somersaulting at the end of his rope like a jumping-jack. For a quarter of a mile up the creek he could hear Miki's entreating protest.

To Challoner the business of the day was not a matter of personal pleasure, nor was it inspired alone by his desire to possess a cub along with Miki. He needed meat, and bear pork thus early in the season would be exceedingly good; and above all else he needed a supply of fat. If he bagged this bear, time would be saved all the rest of the way down to civilization.

It was eight o'clock when he struck the first unmistakably fresh signs of Noozak and Neewa. It was at the point where Noozak had fished four or five days previously, and where they had returned yesterday to feast on the "ripened" catch. Challoner was elated. He was sure that he would find the pair along the creek, and not far distant. The wind was in his favour, and he began to advance with greater caution, his rifle ready for the anticipated moment. For an hour he travelled steadily and quietly, marking every sound and movement ahead of him, and wetting his finger now and then to see if the wind had shifted. After all, it was not so much a matter of human cunning. Everything was in Challoner's favour.

In a wide, flat part of the valley where the creek split itself into a dozen little channels, and the water rippled between sandy bars and over pebbly shallows, Neewa and his mother were nosing about lazily for a breakfast of crawfish. The world had never looked more beautiful to Neewa. The sun made the soft hair on his back fluff up like that of a purring cat. He liked the plash of wet sand under his feet and the singing gush of water against his legs. He liked the sound that was all about him, the breath of the wind, the whispers that came out of the spruce-tops and the cedars, the murmur of water, the Twit-Twit of the rock rabbits, the call of birds; and more than all else the low, grunting talk of his mother.

It was in this sun-bathed sweep of the valley that Noozak caught the first whiff of danger. It came to her in a sudden twist of the wind—the smell of man!

Instantly she was turned into rock. There was still the deep scar in her shoulder which had come, years before, with that same smell of the one enemy she feared. For three summers she had not caught the taint in her nostrils and she had almost forgotten its existence. Now, so suddenly that it paralyzed her, it was warm and terrible in the breath of the wind.

In this moment, too, Neewa seemed to sense the nearness of an appalling danger. Two hundred yards from Challoner he stood a motionless blotch of jet against the white of the sand about him, his eyes on his mother, and his sensitive little nose trying to catch the meaning of the menace in the air.

Then came a thing he had never heard before—a splitting, cracking roar—something that was almost like thunder and yet unlike it; and he saw his mother lurch where she stood and crumple down all at once on her fore legs.

The next moment she was up, with a wild Whoof in her voice that was new to him—a warning for him to fly for his life.

Like all mothers who have known the comradeship and love of a child, Noozak's first thought was of him. Reaching out a paw she gave him a sudden shove, and Neewa legged it wildly for the near-by shelter of the timber. Noozak followed. A second shot came, and close over her head there sped a purring, terrible sound. But Noozak did not hurry. She kept behind Neewa, urging him on even as that pain of a red-hot iron in her groin filled her with agony. They came to the edge of the timber as Challoner's third shot bit under Noozak's feet.

A moment more and they were within the barricade of the timber. Instinct guided Neewa into the thickest part of it, and close behind him Noozak fought with the last of her dying strength to urge him on. In her old brain there was growing a deep and appalling shadow, something that was beginning to cloud her vision so that she could not see, and she knew that at last she had come to the uttermost end of her trail. With twenty years of life behind her, she struggled now for a last few seconds. She stopped Neewa close to a thick cedar, and as she had done many times before she commanded him to climb it. Just once her hot tongue touched his face in a final caress. Then she turned to fight her last great fight.

Straight into the face of Challoner she dragged herself, and fifty feet from the spruce she stopped and waited for him, her head drooped between her shoulders, her sides heaving, her eyes dimming more and more, until at last she sank down with a great sigh, barring the trail of their enemy. For a space, it may be, she saw once more the golden moons and the blazing suns of those twenty years that were gone; it may be that the soft, sweet music of spring came to her again, filled with the old, old song of life, and that Something gracious and painless descended upon her as a final reward for a glorious motherhood on earth.

When Challoner came up she was dead.

From his hiding place in a crotch of the spruce Neewa looked down on the first great tragedy of his life, and the advent of man. The two-legged beast made him cringe deeper into his refuge, and his little heart was near breaking with the terror that had seized upon him. He did not reason. It was by no miracle of mental process that he knew something terrible had happened, and that this tall, two-legged creature was the cause of it. His little eyes were blazing, just over the level of the crotch. He wondered why his mother did not get up and fight when this new enemy came. Frightened as he was he was ready to snarl if she would only wake up—ready to hurry down the tree and help her as he had helped her in the defeat of Makoos, the old he-bear. But not a muscle of Noozak's huge body moved as Challoner bent over her. She was stone dead.

Challoner's face was flushed with exultation. Necessity had made of him a killer. He saw in Noozak a splendid pelt, and a provision of meat that would carry him all the rest of the way to the southland. He leaned his rifle against a tree and began looking about for the cub. Knowledge of the wild told him it would not be far from its mother, and he began looking into the trees and the near-by thickets.

In the shelter of his crotch, screened by the thick branches, Neewa made himself as small as possible during the search. At the end of half an hour Challoner disappointedly gave up his quest, and went back to the creek for a drink before setting himself to the task of skinning Noozak.

No sooner was he gone than Neewa's little head shot up alertly. For a few moments he watched, and then slipped backward down the trunk of the cedar to the ground. He gave his squealing call, but his mother did not move. He went to her and stood beside her motionless head, sniffing the man-tainted air. Then he muzzled her jowl, butted his nose under her neck, and at last nipped her ear—always his last resort in the awakening process. He was puzzled. He whined softly, and climbed upon his mother's big, soft back, and sat there. Into his whine there came a strange note, and then out of his throat there rose a whimpering cry that was like the cry of a child.

Challoner heard that cry as he came back, and something seemed to grip hold of his heart suddenly, and choke him. He had heard children crying like that; and it was the motherless cub!

Creeping up behind a dwarf spruce he looked where Noozak lay dead, and saw Neewa perched on his mother's back. He had killed many things in his time, for it was his business to kill, and to barter in the pelts of creatures that others killed. But he had seen nothing like this before, and he felt all at once as if he had done murder.

"I'm sorry," he breathed softly, "you poor little devil; I'm sorry!"

It was almost a prayer—for forgiveness. Yet there was but one thing to do now. So quietly that Neewa failed to hear him he crept around with the wind and stole up behind. He was within a dozen feet of Neewa before the cub suspected danger. Then it was too late. In a swift rush Challoner was upon him and, before Neewa could leave the back of his mother, had smothered him in the folds of the grub sack.

In all his life Challoner had never experienced a livelier five minutes than the five that followed. Above Neewa's grief and his fear there rose the savage fighting blood of old Soominitik, his father. He clawed and bit and kicked and snarled. In those five minutes he was five little devils all rolled into one, and by the time Challoner had the rope fastened about Neewa's neck, and his fat body chucked into the sack, his hands were scratched and lacerated in a score of places.

In the sack Neewa continued to fight until he was exhausted, while Challoner skinned Noozak and cut from her the meat and fats which he wanted. The beauty of Noozak's pelt brought a glow into his eyes. In it he rolled the meat and fats, and with babiche thong bound the whole into a pack around which he belted the dunnage ends of his shoulder straps. Weighted under the burden of sixty pounds of pelt and meat he picked up his rifle—and Neewa. It had been early afternoon when he left. It was almost sunset when he reached camp. Every foot of the way, until the last half mile, Neewa fought like a Spartan.

Now he lay limp and almost lifeless in his sack, and when Miki came up to smell suspiciously of his prison he made no movement of protest. All smells were alike to him now, and of sounds he made no distinction. Challoner was nearly done for. Every muscle and bone in his body had its ache. Yet in his face, sweaty and grimed, was a grin of pride.

"You plucky little devil," he said, contemplating the limp sack as he loaded his pipe for the first time that afternoon. "You—you plucky little devil!"

He tied the end of Neewa's rope halter to a sapling, and began cautiously to open the grub sack. Then he rolled Neewa out on the ground, and stepped back. In that hour Neewa was willing to accept a truce so far as Challoner was concerned. But it was not Challoner that his half-blinded eyes saw first as he rolled from his bag. It was Miki! And Miki, his awkward body wriggling with the excitement of his curiosity, was almost on the point of smelling of him!

Neewa's little eyes glared. Was that ill-jointed lop-eared offspring of the man-beast an enemy, too? Were those twisting convolutions of this new creature's body and the club-like swing of his tail an invitation to fight? He judged so. Anyway, here was something of his size, and like a flash he was at the end of his rope and on the pup. Miki, a moment before bubbling over with friendship and good cheer, was on his back in an instant, his grotesque legs paddling the air and his yelping cries for help rising in a wild clamour that filled the golden stillness of the evening with an unutterable woe.

Challoner stood dumbfounded. In another moment he would have separated the little fighters, but something happened that stopped him. Neewa, standing squarely over Miki, with Miki's four over-grown paws held aloft as if signalling an unqualified surrender, slowly drew his teeth from the pup's loose hide. Again he saw the man-beast. Instinct, keener than a clumsy reasoning, held him for a few moments without movement, his beady eyes on Challoner. In midair Miki wagged his paws; he whined softly; his hard tail thumped the ground as he pleaded for mercy, and he licked his chops and tried to wriggle, as if to tell Neewa that he had no intention at all to do him harm. Neewa, facing Challoner, snarled defiantly. He drew himself slowly from over Miki. And Miki, afraid to move, still lay on his back with his paws in the air.

Very slowly, a look of wonder in his face, Challoner drew back into the tent and peered through a rent in the canvas.

The snarl left Neewa's face. He looked at the pup. Perhaps away back in some corner of his brain the heritage of instinct was telling him of what he had lost because of brothers and sisters unborn—the comradeship of babyhood, the play of children. And Miki must have sensed the change in the furry little black creature who a moment ago was his enemy. His tail thumped almost frantically, and he swung out his front paws toward Neewa. Then, a little fearful of what might happen, he rolled on his side. Still Neewa did not move. Joyously Miki wriggled.

A moment later, looking through the slit in the canvas, Challoner saw them cautiously smelling noses.

IV

That night came a cold and drizzling rain from out of the north and the east. In the wet dawn Challoner came out to start a fire, and in a hollow under a spruce root he found Miki and Neewa cuddled together, sound asleep.

It was the cub who first saw the man-beast, and for a brief space before the pup roused himself Neewa's shining eyes were fixed on the strange enemy who had so utterly changed his world for him. Exhaustion had made him sleep through the long hours of that first night of captivity, and in sleep he had forgotten many things. But now it all came back to him as he cringed deeper into his shelter under the root, and so softly that only Miki heard him he whimpered for his mother.

It was the whimper that roused Miki. Slowly he untangled himself from the ball into which he had rolled, stretched his long and overgrown legs, and yawned so loudly that the sound reached Challoner's ears. The man turned and saw two pairs of eyes fixed upon him from the sheltered hollow under the root. The pup's one good ear and the other that was half gone stood up alertly, as he greeted his master with the boundless good cheer of an irrepressible comradeship. Challoner's face, wet with the drizzle of the gray skies and bronzed by the wind and storm of fourteen months in the northland, lighted up with a responsive grin, and Miki wriggled forth weaving and twisting himself into grotesque contortions expressive of happiness at being thus directly smiled at by his master.

With all the room under the root left to him Neewa pulled himself back until only his round head was showing, and from this fortress of temporary safety his bright little eyes glared forth at his mother's murderer.

Vividly the tragedy of yesterday was before him again—the warm, sun-filled creek bottom in which he and Noozak, his mother, were hunting a breakfast of crawfish when the man-beast came; the crash of strange thunder, their flight into the timber, and the end of it all when his mother turned to confront their enemy. And yet it was not the death of his mother that remained with him most poignantly this morning. It was the memory of his own terrific fight with the white man, and his struggle afterward in the black and suffocating depths of the bag in which Challoner had brought him to his camp. Even now Challoner was looking at the scratches on his hands. He advanced a few steps, and grinned down at Neewa, just as he had grinned good-humouredly at Miki, the angular pup.

Neewa's little eyes blazed.

"I told you last night that I was sorry," said Challoner, speaking as if to one of his own kind.

In several ways Challoner was unusual, an out-of-the-ordinary type in the northland. He believed, for instance, in a certain specific psychology of the animal mind, and had proven to his own satisfaction that animals treated and conversed with in a matter-of-fact human way frequently developed an understanding which he, in his unscientific way, called reason.

"I told you I was sorry," he repeated, squatting on his heels within a yard of the root from under which Neewa's eyes were glaring at him, "and I am. I'm sorry I killed your mother. But we had to have meat and fat. Besides, Miki and I are going to make it up to you. We're going to take you along with us down to the Girl, and if you don't learn to love her you're the meanest, lowest-down little cuss in all creation and don't deserve a mother. You and Miki are going to be brothers. His mother is dead, too—plum starved to death, which is worse than dying with a bullet in your lung. And I found Miki just as I found you, hugging up close to her an' crying as if there wasn't any world left for him. So cheer up, and give us your paw. Let's shake!"

Challoner held out his hand. Neewa was as motionless as a stone. A few moments before he would have snarled and bared his teeth. But now he was dead still. This was by all odds the strangest beast he had ever seen. Yesterday it had not harmed him, except to put him into the bag. And now it did not offer to harm him. More than that, the talk it made was not unpleasant, or threatening. His eyes took in Miki. The pup had squeezed himself squarely between Challoner's knees and was looking at him in a puzzled, questioning sort of way, as if to ask: "Why don't you come out from under that root and help get breakfast?"

Challoner's hand came nearer, and Neewa crowded himself back until there was not another inch of room for him to fill. Then the miracle happened. The man-beast's paw touched his head. It sent a strange and terrible thrill through him. Yet it did not hurt. If he had not wedged himself in so tightly he would have scratched and bitten. But he could do neither.

Slowly Challoner worked his fingers to the loose hide at the back of Neewa's neck. Miki, surmising that something momentous was about to happen, watched the proceedings with popping eyes. Then Challoner's fingers closed and the next instant he dragged Neewa forth and held him at arm's length, kicking and squirming, and setting up such a bawling that in sheer sympathy Miki raised his voice and joined in the agonized orgy of sound. Half a minute later Challoner had Neewa once more in the prison-sack, but this time he left the cub's head protruding, and drew in the mouth of the sack closely about his neck, fastening it securely with a piece of babiche string. Thus three quarters of Neewa was imprisoned in the sack, with only his head sticking out. He was a cub in a poke.

Leaving the cub to roll and squirm in protest Challoner went about the business of getting breakfast. For once Miki found a proceeding more interesting than that operation, and he hovered about Neewa as he struggled and bawled, trying vainly to offer him some assistance in the matter of sympathy. Finally Neewa lay still, and Miki sat down close beside him and eyed his master with serious questioning if not actual disapprobation.

The gray sky was breaking with the promise of the sun when Challoner was ready to renew his long journey into the southland. He packed his canoe, leaving Neewa and Miki until the last. In the bow of the canoe he made a soft nest of the skin taken from the cub's mother. Then he called Miki and tied the end of a worn rope around his neck, after which he fastened the other end of this rope around the neck of Neewa. Thus he had the cub and the pup on the same yard-long halter. Taking each of the twain by the scruff of the neck he carried them to the canoe and placed them in the nest he had made of Noozak's hide.

"Now you youngsters be good," he warned. "We're going to aim at forty miles to-day to make up for the time we lost yesterday."

As the canoe shot out a shaft of sunlight broke through the sky low in the east.

V

During the first few moments in which the canoe moved swiftly over the surface of the lake an amazing change had taken place in Neewa. Challoner did not see it, and Miki was unconscious of it. But every fibre in Neewa's body was atremble, and his heart was thumping as it had pounded on that glorious day of the fight between his mother and the old he-bear. It seemed to him that everything that he had lost was coming back to him, and that all would be well very soon—FOR HE SMELLED HIS MOTHER! And then he discovered that the scent of her was warm and strong in the furry black mass under his feet, and he smothered himself down in it, flat on his plump little belly, and peered at Challoner over his paws.

It was hard for him to understand—the man-beast back there, sending the canoe through the water, and under him his mother, warm and soft, but so deadly still! He could not keep the whimper out of his throat—his low and grief-filled call for HER. And there was no answer, except Miki's responsive whine, the crying of one child for another. Neewa's mother did not move. She made no sound. And he could see nothing of her but her black and furry skin—without head, without feet, without the big, bald paws he had loved to tickle, and the ears he had loved to nip. There was nothing of her but the patch of black skin—and the SMELL.

But a great comfort warmed his frightened little soul. He felt the protecting nearness of an unconquerable and abiding force and in the first of the warm sunshine his back fluffed up, and he thrust his brown nose between his paws and into his mother's fur. Miki, as if vainly striving to solve the mystery of his new-found chum, was watching him closely from between his own fore-paws. In his comical head—adorned with its one good ear and its one bad one, and furthermore beautified by the outstanding whiskers inherited from his Airedale ancestor—he was trying to come to some sort of an understanding. At the outset he had accepted Neewa as a friend and a comrade—and Neewa had thanklessly given him a good mauling for his trouble. That much Miki could forgive and forget. What he could not forgive was the utter lack of regard which Neewa seemed to possess for him. His playful antics had gained no recognition from the cub. When he had barked and hopped about, flattening and contorting himself in warm invitation for

JAMES OLIVER CURWOOD

him to join in a game of tag or a wrestling match, Neewa had simply stared at him like an idiot. He was wondering, perhaps, if Neewa would enjoy anything besides a fight. It was a long time before he decided to make another experiment.

It was, as a matter of fact, halfway between breakfast and noon. In all that time Neewa had scarcely moved, and Miki was finding himself bored to death. The discomfort of last night's storm was only a memory, and overhead there was a sun unshadowed by cloud. More than an hour before Challoner's canoe had left the lake, and was now in the clear-running water of a stream that was making its way down the southward slope of the divide between Jackson's Knee and the Shamattawa. It was a new stream to Challoner, fed by the large lake above, and guarding himself against the treachery of waterfall and rapid he kept a keen lookout ahead. For a matter of half an hour the water had been growing steadily swifter, and Challoner was satisfied that before very long he would be compelled to make a portage. A little later he heard ahead of him the low and steady murmur which told him he was approaching a danger zone. As he shot around the next bend, hugging fairly close to shore, he saw, four or five hundred yards below him, a rock-frothed and boiling maelstrom of water.

Swiftly his eyes measured the situation. The rapids ran between an almost precipitous shore on one side and a deep forest on the other. He saw at a glance that it was the forest side over which he must make the portage, and this was the shore opposite him and farthest away. Swinging his canoe at a 45-degree angle he put all the strength of body and arms into the sweep of his paddle. There would be just time to reach the other shore before the current became dangerous. Above the sweep of the rapids he could now hear the growling roar of a waterfall below.

It was at this unfortunate moment that Miki decided to venture one more experiment with Neewa. With a friendly yip he swung out one of his paws. Now Miki's paw, for a pup, was monstrously big, and his foreleg was long and lanky, so that when the paw landed squarely on the end of Neewa's nose it was like the swing of a prize-fighter's glove. The unexpectedness of it was a further decisive feature in the situation; and, on top of this, Miki swung his other paw around like a club and caught Neewa a jolt in the eye. This was too much, even from a friend, and with a sudden snarl Neewa bounced out of his nest and clinched with the pup.

Now the fact was that Miki, who had so ingloriously begged for mercy in their first scrimmage, came of fighting stock himself. Mix the blood of a Mackenzie hound—which is the biggest-footed, biggest-shouldered, most powerful dog in the northland—with the blood of a Spitz and an Airedale and something is bound to come of it. While the Mackenzie dog, with his ox-like strength, is peaceable and good-humoured in all sorts of weather, there is a good deal of the devil in the northern Spitz and Airedale and it is a question which likes a fight the best. And all at once good-humoured little Miki felt the devil rising in him. This time he did not yap for mercy. He met Neewa's jaws, and in two seconds they were staging a first-class fight on the bit of precarious footing in the prow of the canoe.

Vainly Challoner yelled at them as he paddled desperately to beat out the danger of the rapids. Neewa and Miki were too absorbed to hear him. Miki's four paws were paddling the air again, but this time his sharp teeth were firmly fixed in the loose hide under Neewa's neck, and with his paws he continued to kick and bat in a way that promised effectively to pummel the wind out of Neewa had not the thing happened which Challoner feared. Still in a clinch they rolled off the prow of the canoe into the swirling current of the stream.

For ten seconds or so they utterly disappeared. Then they bobbed up, a good fifty feet below him, their heads close together as they sped swiftly toward the doom that awaited them, and a choking cry broke from Challoner's lips. He was powerless to save them, and in his cry was the anguish of real grief. For many weeks Miki had been his only chum and comrade.

Held together by the yard-long rope to which they were fastened, Miki and Neewa swept into the frothing turmoil of the rapids. For Miki it was the kindness of fate that had inspired his master to fasten him to the same rope with Neewa. Miki, at three months of age—weight, fourteen pounds—was about 80 per cent. bone and only a half of 1 per cent. fat; while Neewa, weight thirteen pounds, was about 90 per cent. fat. Therefore Miki had the floating capacity of a small anchor, while Neewa was a first-class life-preserver, and almost unsinkable.

In neither of the youngsters was there a yellow streak. Both were of fighting stock, and, though Miki was under water most of the time during their first hundred-yard dash through the rapids, never for an instant did he give up the struggle to keep his nose in the air. Sometimes he was on his back and sometimes on his belly; but no matter what his

JAMES OLIVER CURWOOD

position, he kept his four overgrown paws going like paddles. To an extent this helped Neewa in the heroic fight he was making to keep from shipping too much water himself. Had he been alone his ten or eleven pounds of fat would have carried him down-stream like a toy balloon covered with fur, but, with the fourteen-pound drag around his neck, the problem of not going under completely was a serious one. Half a dozen times he did disappear for an instant when some undertow caught Miki and dragged him down—head, tail, legs, and all. But Neewa always rose again, his four fat legs working for dear life.

Then came the waterfall. By this time Miki had become accustomed to travelling under water, and the full horror of the new cataclysm into which they were plunged was mercifully lost to him. His paws had almost ceased their motion. He was still conscious of the roar in his ears, but the affair was less unpleasant than it was at the beginning. In fact, he was drowning. To Neewa the pleasant sensations of a painless death were denied. No cub in the world was wider awake than he when the final catastrophe came. His head was well above water and he was clearly possessed of all his senses. Then the river itself dropped out from under him and he shot down in an avalanche of water, feeling no longer the drag of Miki's weight at his neck.

How deep the pool was at the bottom of the waterfall Challoner might have guessed quite accurately. Could Neewa have expressed an opinion of his own, he would have sworn that it was a mile. Miki was past the stage of making estimates, or of caring whether it was two feet or two leagues. His paws had ceased to operate and he had given himself up entirely to his fate. But Neewa came up again, and Miki followed, like a bobber. He was about to gasp his last gasp when the force of the current, as it swung out of the whirlpool, flung Neewa upon a bit of partly submerged driftage, and in a wild and strenuous effort to make himself safe Neewa dragged Miki's head out of water so that the pup hung at the edge of the driftage like a hangman's victim at the end of his rope.

VI

It is doubtful whether in the few moments that followed, any clear-cut mental argument passed through Neewa's head. It is too much to suppose that he deliberately set about assisting the half-dead and almost unconscious Miki from his precarious position. His sole ambition was to get himself where it was safe and dry, and to do this he of necessity had to drag the pup with him. So Neewa tugged at the end of his rope, digging his sharp little claws into the driftwood, and as he advanced Miki was dragged up head foremost out of the cold and friendless stream. It was a simple process. Neewa reached a log around which the water was eddying, and there he flattened himself down and hung on as he had never hung to anything else in his life. The log was entirely hidden from shore by a dense growth of brushwood. Otherwise, ten minutes later Challoner would have seen them.

As it was, Miki had not sufficiently recovered either to smell or hear his master when Challoner came to see if there was a possibility of his small comrade being alive. And Neewa only hugged the log more tightly. He had seen enough of the man-beast to last him for the remainder of his life. It was half an hour before Miki began to gasp, and cough, and gulp up water, and for the first time since their scrap in the canoe the cub began to take a live interest in him. In another ten minutes Miki raised his head and looked about him. At that Neewa gave a tug on the rope, as if to advise him that it was time to get busy if they were expected to reach shore. And Miki, drenched and forlorn, resembling more a starved bone than a thing of skin and flesh, actually made an effort to wag his tail when he saw Neewa.

He was still in a couple of inches of water, and with a hopeful eye on the log upon which Neewa was squatted he began to work his wobbly legs toward it. It was a high log, and a dry log, and when Miki reached it his unlucky star was with him again. Cumbrously he sprawled himself against it, and as he scrambled and scraped with his four awkward legs to get up alongside Neewa he gave to the log the slight push which it needed to set it free of the sunken driftage. Slowly at first the eddying current carried one end of the log away from its pier. Then the edge of the main current caught at it, viciously—and so suddenly that Miki almost lost his precarious footing, the log gave a twist, righted itself, and began, to scud down stream at a speed that would have made

Challoner hug his breath had he been in their position with his faithful canoe.

In fact, Challoner was at this very moment portaging the rapids below the waterfall. To have set his canoe in them where Miki and Neewa were gloriously sailing he would have considered an inexcusable hazard, and as a matter of safety he was losing the better part of a couple of hours by packing his outfit through the forest to a point half a mile below. That half mile was to the cub and the pup a show which was destined to live in their memories for as long as they were alive.

They were facing each other about amidships of the log, Neewa flattened tight, his sharp claws dug in like hooks, and his little brown eyes half starting from his head. It would have taken a crowbar to wrench him from the log. But with Miki it was an open question from the beginning whether he would weather the storm. He had no claws that he could dig into the wood, and it was impossible for him to use his clumsy legs as Neewa used his—like two pairs of human arms. All he could do was to balance himself, slipping this way or that as the log rolled or swerved in its course, sometimes lying across it and sometimes lengthwise, and every moment with the jaws of uncertainty open wide for him. Neewa's eyes never left him for an instant. Had they been gimlets they would have bored holes. From the acuteness of this life-and-death stare one would have given Neewa credit for understanding that his own personal safety depended not so much upon his claws and his hug as upon Miki's seamanship. If Miki went overboard there would be left but one thing for him to do—and that would be to follow.

The log, being larger and heavier at one end than at the other, swept on without turning broadside, and with the swiftness and appearance of a huge torpedo. While Neewa's back was turned toward the horror of frothing water and roaring rock behind him, Miki, who was facing it, lost none of its spectacular beauty. Now and then the log shot into one of the white masses of foam and for an instant or two would utterly disappear; and at these intervals Miki would hold his breath and close his eyes while Neewa dug his toes in still deeper. Once the log grazed a rock. Six inches more and they would have been without a ship. Their trip was not half over before both cub and pup looked like two round balls of lather out of which their eyes peered wildly.

Swiftly the roar of the cataract was left behind; the huge rocks around which the current boiled and twisted with a ferocious snarling became fewer; there came open spaces in which the log floated smoothly and without convulsions, and then, at last, the quiet and placid flow of calm water. Not until then did the two balls of suds make a move. For the first time Neewa saw the whole of the thing they had passed through, and Miki, looking down stream, saw the quiet shores again, the deep forest, and the stream aglow with the warm sun. He drew in a breath that filled his whole body and let it out again with a sigh of relief so deep and sincere that it blew out a scatter of foam from the ends of his nose and whiskers. For the first time he became conscious of his own discomfort. One of his hind legs was twisted under him, and a foreleg was under his chest. The smoothness of the water and the nearness of the shores gave him confidence, and he proceeded to straighten himself. Unlike Neewa he was an experienced Voyageur. For more than a month he had travelled steadily with Challoner in his canoe, and of ordinarily decent water he was unafraid. So he perked up a little, and offered Neewa a congratulatory yip that was half a whine.

But Neewa's education had travelled along another line, and while his experience in a canoe had been confined to that day he did know what a log was. He knew from more than one adventure of his own that a log in the water is the next thing to a live thing, and that its capacity for playing evil jokes was beyond any computation that he had ever been able to make. That was where Miki's store of knowledge was fatally defective. Inasmuch as the log had carried them safely through the worst stretch of water he had ever seen he regarded it in the light of a first-class canoe—with the exception that it was unpleasantly rounded on top. But this little defect did not worry him. To Neewa's horror he sat up boldly, and looked about him.

Instinctively the cub hugged the log still closer, while Miki was seized with an overwhelming desire to shake from himself the mass of suds in which, with the exception of the end of his tail and his eyes, he was completely swathed. He had often shaken himself in the canoe; why not here? Without either asking or answering the question he did it.

Like the trap of a gibbet suddenly sprung by the hangman, the log instantly responded by turning half over. Without so much as a wail Miki was off like a shot, hit the water with a deep and solemn Chug, and once more disappeared as completely as if he had been made of lead.

Finding himself completely submerged for the first time, Neewa hung on gloriously, and when the log righted itself again he was tenaciously hugging his old place, all the froth washed from him. He looked for Miki—but Miki was gone. And then he felt once more that choking drag on his neck! Of necessity, because his head was pulled in the direction of the rope, he saw where the rope disappeared in the water. But there was no Miki. The pup was down too far for Neewa to see. With the drag growing heavier and heavier—for here there was not much current to help Miki along—Neewa hung on like grim death. If he had let go, and had joined Miki in the water, the good fortune which was turning their way would have been missed. For Miki, struggling well under water, was serving both as an anchor and a rudder; slowly the log shifted its course, was caught in a beach-eddy, and drifted in close to a muddy bank.

With one wild leap Neewa was ashore. Feeling the earth under his feet he started to run, and the result was that Miki came up slowly through the mire and spread himself out like an overgrown crustacean while he got the wind back into his lungs. Neewa, sensing the fact that for a few moments his comrade was physically unfit for travel, shook himself, and waited. Miki picked up quickly. Within five minutes he was on his feet shaking himself so furiously that Neewa became the centre of a shower of mud and water.

Had they remained where they were, Challoner would have found them an hour or so later, for he paddled that way, close inshore, looking for their bodies. It may be that the countless generations of instinct back of Neewa warned him of that possibility, for within a quarter of an hour after they had landed he was leading the way into the forest, and Miki was following. It was a new adventure for the pup.

But Neewa began to recover his good cheer. For him the forest was home even if his mother was missing. After his maddening experiences with Miki and the man-beast the velvety touch of the soft pine-needles under his feet and the familiar smells of the silent places filled him with a growing joy. He was back in his old trails. He sniffed the air and pricked up his ears, thrilled by the enlivening sensations of knowing that he was once more the small master of his own destiny. It was a new forest, but Neewa was undisturbed by this fact. All forests were alike to him, inasmuch as several hundred thousand square miles were included in his domain and it was impossible for him to landmark them all.

With Miki it was different. He not only began to miss Challoner and the river, but became more and more disturbed the farther Neewa led him into the dark and mysterious depths of the timber. At last he decided to set up a vigorous protest, and in line with this decision he braced himself so suddenly that Neewa, coming to the end of the rope, flopped over on his back with an astonished grunt. Seizing his advantage Miki turned, and tugging with the horse-like energy of his Mackenzie father he started back toward the river, dragging Neewa after him for a space of ten or fifteen feet before the cub succeeded in regaining his feet.

Then the battle began. With their bottoms braced and their forefeet digging into the soft earth, they pulled on the rope in opposite directions until their necks stretched and their eyes began to pop. Neewa's pull was steady and unexcited, while Miki, dog-like, yanked and convulsed himself in sudden backward jerks that made Neewa give way an inch at a time. It was, after all, only a question as to which possessed the most enduring neck. Under Neewa's fat there was as yet little real physical strength. Miki had him handicapped there. Under the pup's loose hide and his overgrown bones there was a lot of pull, and after bracing himself heroically for another dozen feet Neewa gave up the contest and followed in the direction chosen by Miki.

While the instincts of Neewa's breed would have taken him back to the river as straight as a die, Miki's intentions were better than was his sense of orientation. Neewa followed in a sweeter temper when he found that his companion was making an unreasonable circle which was taking them a little more slowly, but just as surely, away from the danger-ridden stream. At the end of another quarter of an hour Miki was utterly lost; he sat down on his rump, looked at Neewa, and confessed as much—with a low whine. Neewa did not move. His sharp little eyes were fixed suddenly on an object that hung to a low bush half a dozen paces from them. Before the man-beast's appearance the cub had spent three quarters of his time in eating, but since yesterday morning he had not swallowed so much as a bug. He was completely empty, and the object he saw hanging to the bush set every salivary gland in his mouth working. It was a wasp's nest. Many times in his young life he had seen Noozak, his mother, go up to nests like that, tear them down, crush them under her big paw, and then invite him to the feast of dead wasps within. For at least a month wasps had been included in his daily fare, and they were as good as anything he knew of. He approached the nest; Miki followed. When they were within three feet of it Miki began to take notice of a very distinct and peculiarly disquieting buzzing sound. Neewa was not at all alarmed; judging the distance of the nest from the ground, he rose on his hind feet, raised his arms, and gave it a fatal tug.

JAMES OLIVER CURWOOD

Instantly the drone which Miki had heard changed into the angry buzzing of a saw. Quick as a flash Neewa's mother would have had the nest under her paws and the life crushed out of it, while Neewa's tug had only served partly to dislodge the home of Ahmoo and his dangerous tribe. And it happened that Ahmoo was at home with three quarters of his warriors. Before Neewa could give the nest a second tug they were piling out of it in a cloud and suddenly a wild yell of agony rose out of Miki. Ahmoo himself had landed on the end of the dog's nose. Neewa made no sound, but stood for a moment swiping at his face with both paws, while Miki, still yelling, ran the end of his crucified nose into the ground. In another moment every fighter in Ahmoo's army was busy. Suddenly setting up a bawling on his own account Neewa turned tail to the nest and ran. Miki was not a hair behind him. In every square inch of his tender hide he felt the red-hot thrust of a needle. It was Neewa that made the most noise. His voice was one continuous bawl, and to this bass Miki's soprano wailing added the touch which would have convinced any passing Indian that the loup-garou devils were having a dance.

Now that their foes were in disorderly flight the wasps, who are rather a chivalrous enemy, would have returned to their upset fortress had not Miki, in his mad flight, chosen one side of a small sapling and Neewa the other—a misadventure that stopped them with a force almost sufficient to break their necks. Thereupon a few dozen of Ahmoo's rear guard started in afresh. With his fighting blood at last aroused, Neewa swung out and caught Miki where there was almost no hair on his rump. Already half blinded, and so wrought up with pain and terror that he had lost all sense of judgment or understanding, Miki believed that the sharp dig of Neewa's razor-like claws was a deeper thrust than usual of the buzzing horrors that overwhelmed him, and with a final shriek he proceeded to throw a fit.

It was the fit that saved them. In his maniacal contortions he swung around to Neewa's side of the sapling, when, with their halter once more free from impediment, Neewa bolted for safety. Miki followed, yelping at every jump. No longer did Neewa feel a horror of the river. The instinct of his kind told him that he wanted water, and wanted it badly. As straight as Challoner might have set his course by a compass he headed for the stream, but he had proceeded only a few hundred feet when they came upon a tiny creek across which either of them could have jumped. Neewa jumped into the water, which was four or five inches deep, and for the first time in his life Miki voluntarily took a plunge. For a long time they lay in the cooling rill.

The light of day was dim and hazy before Miki's eyes, and he was beginning to swell from the tip of his nose to the end of his bony tail. Neewa, being so much fat, suffered less. He could still see, and, as the painful hours passed, a number of things were adjusting themselves in his brain. All this had begun with the man-beast. It was the man-beast who had taken his mother from him. It was the man-beast who had chucked him into the dark sack, and it was the man-beast who had FASTENED THE ROPE AROUND HIS NECK. Slowly the fact was beginning to impinge itself upon him that the rope was to blame for everything.

After a long time they dragged themselves out of the rivulet and found a soft, dry hollow at the foot of a big tree. Even to Neewa, who had the use of his eyes, it was growing dark in the deep forest. The sun was far in the west. And the air was growing chilly. Flat on his belly, with his swollen head between his fore paws, Miki whined plaintively.

Again and again Neewa's eyes went to the rope as the big thought developed itself in his head. He whined. It was partly a yearning for his mother, partly a response to Miki. He drew closer to the pup, filled with the irresistible desire for comradeship. After all, it was not Miki who was to blame. It was the man-beast—and THE ROPE!

The gloom of evening settled more darkly about them, and snuggling himself still closer to the pup Neewa drew the rope between his fore paws. With a little snarl he set his teeth in it. And then, steadily, he began to chew. Now and then he growled, and in the growl there was a peculiarly communicative note, as if he wished to say to Miki:

"Don't you see?—I'm chewing this thing in two. I'll have it done by morning. Cheer up! There's surely a better day coming."

VII

The morning after their painful experience with the wasp's nest, Neewa and Miki rose on four pairs of stiff and swollen legs to greet a new day in the deep and mysterious forest into which the accident of the previous day had thrown them. The spirit of irrepressible youth was upon them, and, though Miki was so swollen from the stings of the wasps that his lank body and overgrown legs were more grotesque than ever, he was in no way daunted from the quest of further adventure.

The pup's face was as round as a moon, and his head was puffed up until Neewa might reasonably have had a suspicion that it was on the point of exploding. But Miki's eyes—as much as could be seen of them—were as bright as ever, and his one good ear and his one half ear stood up hopefully as he waited for the cub to give some sign of what they were going to do. The poison in his system no longer gave him discomfort. He felt several sizes too large—but, otherwise, quite well.

Neewa, because of his fat, exhibited fewer effects of his battle with the wasps. His one outstanding defect was an entirely closed eye. With the other, wide open and alert, he looked about him. In spite of his one bad eye and his stiff legs he was inspired with the optimism of one who at last sees fortune turning his way. He was rid of the man-beast, who had killed his mother; the forests were before him again, open and inviting, and the rope with which Challoner had tied him and Miki together he had successfully gnawed in two during the night. Having dispossessed himself of at least two evils it would not have surprised him much if he had seen Noozak, his mother, coming up from out of the shadows of the trees. Thought of her made him whine. And Miki, facing the vast loneliness of his new world, and thinking of his master, whined in reply.

Both were hungry. The amazing swiftness with which their misfortunes had descended upon them had given them no time in which to eat. To Miki the change was more than astonishing; it was overwhelming, and he held his breath in anticipation of some new evil while Neewa scanned the forest about them.

As if assured by this survey that everything was right, Neewa turned his back to the sun, which had been his mother's custom, and set out.

Miki followed. Not until then did he discover that every joint in his body had apparently disappeared. His neck was stiff, his legs were like stilts, and five times in as many minutes he stubbed his clumsy toes and fell down in his efforts to keep up with the cub. On top of this his eyes were so nearly closed that his vision was bad, and the fifth time he stumbled he lost sight of Neewa entirely, and sent out a protesting wail. Neewa stopped and began prodding with his nose under a rotten log. When Miki came up Neewa was flat on his belly, licking up a colony of big red vinegar ants as fast as he could catch them. Miki studied the proceeding for some moments. It soon dawned upon him that Neewa was eating something, but for the life of him he couldn't make out what it was. Hungrily he nosed close to Neewa's foraging snout. He licked with his tongue where Neewa licked, and he got only dirt. And all the time Neewa was giving his jolly little grunts of satisfaction. It was ten minutes before he hunted out the last ant and went on.

A little later they came to a small open space where the ground was wet, and after sniffing about a bit, and focussing his one good eye here and there, Neewa suddenly began digging. Very shortly he drew out of the ground a white object about the size of a man's thumb and began to crunch it ravenously between his jaws. Miki succeeded in capturing a fair sized bit of it. Disappointment followed fast. The thing was like wood; after rolling it in his mouth a few times he dropped it in disgust, and Neewa finished the remnant of the root with a thankful grunt.

They proceeded. For two heartbreaking hours Miki followed at Neewa's heels, the void in his stomach increasing as the swelling in his body diminished. His hunger was becoming a torture. Yet not a bit to eat could he find, while Neewa at every few steps apparently discovered something to devour. At the end of the two hours the cub's bill of fare had grown to considerable proportions. It included, among other things, half a dozen green and black beetles; numberless bugs, both hard and soft; whole colonies of red and black ants; several white grubs dug out of the heart of decaying logs; a handful of snails; a young frog; the egg of a ground-plover that had failed to hatch; and, in the vegetable line, the roots of two camas and one skunk cabbage. Now and then he pulled down tender poplar shoots and nipped the ends off. Likewise he nibbled spruce and balsam gum whenever he found it, and occasionally added to his breakfast a bit of tender grass.

A number of these things Miki tried. He would have eaten the frog, but Neewa was ahead of him there. The spruce and balsam gum clogged up his teeth and almost made him vomit because of its bitterness. Between a snail and a stone he could find little difference, and as the one bug he tried happened to be that asafoetida-like creature known as a stink-bug he made no further efforts in that direction. He also bit off a tender tip from a ground-shoot, but instead of a young poplar it was Fox-bite, and shrivelled up his tongue for a quarter of an hour. At last he arrived at the conclusion that, up to date, the one thing in Neewa's menu that he COULD eat was grass.

In the face of his own starvation his companion grew happier as he added to the strange collection in his stomach. In fact, Neewa considered himself in clover and was grunting his satisfaction continually, especially as his bad eye was beginning to open and he could see things better. Half a dozen times when he found fresh ant nests he invited Miki to the feast with excited little squeals. Until noon Miki followed like a faithful satellite at his heels. The end came when Neewa deliberately dug into a nest inhabited by four huge bumble-bees, smashed them all, and ate them.

From that moment something impressed upon Miki that he must do his own hunting. With the thought came a new thrill. His eyes were fairly open now, and much of the stiffness had gone from his legs. The blood of his Mackenzie father and of his half Spitz and half Airedale mother rose up in him in swift and immediate demand, and he began to quest about for himself. He found a warm scent, and poked about until a partridge went up with a tremendous thunder of wings. It startled him, but added to the thrill. A few minutes later, nosing under a pile of brush, he came face to face with his dinner.

It was Wahboo, the baby rabbit. Instantly Miki was at him, and had a firm hold at the back of Wahboo's back. Neewa, hearing the smashing of the brush and the squealing of the rabbit, stopped catching ants and hustled toward the scene of action. The squealing ceased quickly and Miki backed himself out and faced Neewa with Wahboo held triumphantly in his jaws. The young rabbit had already given his last kick, and with a fierce show of growling Miki began tearing the fur off. Neewa edged in, grunting affably. Miki snarled more fiercely. Neewa, undaunted, continued to express his overwhelming regard for Miki in low and supplicating grunts—and smelled the rabbit. The snarl in Miki's throat died away. He may have remembered that Neewa had invited him more than once to partake of his ants and bugs. Together they ate the rabbit. Not until the last bit of flesh and the last tender bone were gone did the feast end, and then Neewa sat back on his round bottom and stuck out his little red tongue for the first time since he had lost his mother. It was the cub sign of a full stomach and a blissful mind. He could see nothing to be more desired at the present time than a nap, and stretching himself languidly he began looking about for a tree.

Miki, on the other hand, was inspired to new action by the pleasurable sensation of being comfortably filled. Inasmuch as Neewa chewed his food very carefully, while Miki, paying small attention to mastication, swallowed it in chunks, the pup had succeeded in getting away with about four fifths of the rabbit. So he was no longer hungry. But he was more keenly alive to his changed environment than at any time since he and Neewa had fallen out of Challoner's canoe into the rapids. For the first time he had killed, and for the first time he had tasted warm blood, and the combination added to his existence an excitement that was greater than any desire he might have possessed to lie down in a sunny spot and sleep. Now that he had learned the game, the hunting instinct trembled in every fibre of his small being. He would have gone on hunting until his legs gave way under him if Neewa had not found a napping-place.

Astonished half out of his wits he watched Neewa as he leisurely climbed the trunk of a big poplar. He had seen squirrels climb trees—just as he had seen birds fly—but Neewa's performance held him breathless; and not until the cub had stretched himself out comfortably in a crotch did Miki express himself. Then he gave an incredulous yelp, sniffed at the butt of the tree, and made a half-hearted experiment at the thing himself. One flop on his back convinced him that Neewa was the tree-climber of the partnership. Chagrined, he wandered back fifteen or twenty feet and sat down to study the situation. He could not perceive that Neewa had any special business up the tree. Certainly he was not hunting for bugs. He yelped half a dozen times, but Neewa made no answer. At last he gave it up and flopped himself down with a disconsolate whine.

But it was not to sleep. He was ready and anxious to go on. He wanted to explore still further the mysterious and fascinating depths of the forest. He no longer felt the strange fear that had been upon him before he killed the rabbit. In two minutes under the brush-heap Nature had performed one of her miracles of education. In those two minutes Miki had risen out of whimpering puppyhood to new power and understanding. He had passed that elemental stage which his companionship with Challoner had prolonged. He had KILLED, and the hot thrill of it set fire to every instinct that was in him. In the half hour during which he lay flat on his belly, his head alert and listening, while Neewa slept, he passed half way from puppyhood to dogdom. He would never know that Hela, his Mackenzie hound father, was the mightiest hunter in all the reaches of the Little Fox country, and that alone he had torn down a bull caribou. But he FELT it. There was something insistent and demanding in the call. And because he was answering that call, and listening eagerly to the whispering voices of the forest, his quick ears caught the low, chuckling monotone of Kawook, the porcupine.

Miki lay very still. A moment later he heard the soft clicking of quills, and then Kawook came out in the open and stood up on his hind feet in a patch of sunlight.

For thirteen years Kawook had lived undisturbed in this particular part of the wilderness, and in his old age he weighed thirty pounds if he weighed an ounce. On this afternoon, coming for his late dinner, he was feeling even more than usually happy. His eyesight at best was dim. Nature had never intended him to see very far, and had therefore quilted him heavily with the barbed shafts of his protecting armour. Thirty feet away he was entirely oblivious of Miki, at least apparently so; and Miki hugged the ground closer, warned by the swiftly developing instinct within him that here was a creature it would be unwise to attack.

For perhaps a minute Kawook stood up, chuckling his tribal song without any visible movement of his body. He stood profile to Miki, like a fat alderman. He was so fat that his stomach bulged out in front like the half of a balloon, and over this stomach his hands were folded in a peculiarly human way, so that he looked more like an old she-porcupine than a master in his tribe.

It was not until then that Miki observed Iskwasis, the young female porcupine, who had poked herself slyly out from under a bush near Kawook. In spite of his years the red thrill of romance was not yet gone from the old fellow's bones, and he immediately started to give an exhibition of his good breeding and elegance. He began with his ludicrous love-making dance, hopping from one foot to the other until his fat stomach shook, and chuckling louder than ever. The charms of Iskwasis were indeed sufficient to turn the head of an older beau than Kawook. She was a distinctive blonde; in other words, one of those unusual creatures of her kind, an albino. Her nose was pink, the palms of her little feet were pink, and each of her pretty pink eyes was set in an iris of sky-blue. It was evident that she did not regard old Kawook's passion-dance with favour and sensing this fact Kawook changed his tactics and falling on all four feet began to chase his spiky tail as if he had suddenly gone mad. When he stopped, and looked to see what effect he had made he was clearly knocked out by the fact that Iskwasis had disappeared.

For another minute he sat stupidly, without making a sound. Then to Miki's consternation he started straight for the tree in which Neewa was sleeping. As a matter of fact, it was Kawook's dinner-tree, and he began climbing it, talking to himself all the time. Miki's hair began to stand on end. He did not know that Kawook, like all his kind, was the best-natured fellow in the world, and had never harmed anything in his life unless assaulted first. Lacking this knowledge he set up a sudden frenzy of barking to warn Neewa.

Neewa roused himself slowly, and when he opened his eyes he was looking into a spiky face that sent him into a convulsion of alarm. With a suddenness that came within an ace of toppling him from his crotch he swung over and scurried higher up the tree. Kawook was not at all excited. Now that Iskwasis was gone he was entirely absorbed in the anticipation of his dinner. He continued to clamber slowly upward, and at this the horrified Neewa backed himself out on a limb in order that Kawook might have an unobstructed trail up the tree.

Unfortunately for Neewa it was on this limb that Kawook had eaten his last meal, and he began working himself out on it, still apparently oblivious of the fact that the cub was on the same branch. At this Miki sent up such a series of shrieking yelps from below that Kawook seemed at last to realize that something unusual was going on. He peered down at Miki who was making vain efforts to jump up the trunk of the tree; then he turned and, for the first time, contemplated Neewa with some sign of interest. Neewa was hugging the limb with both forearms and both hind legs. To retreat another foot on the branch that was already bending dangerously under his weight seemed impossible.

It was at this point that Kawook began to scold fiercely. With a final frantic yelp Miki sat back on his haunches and watched the thrilling drama above him. A little at a time Kawook advanced, and inch by inch Neewa retreated, until at last he rolled clean over and was hanging with his back toward the ground. It was then that Kawook ceased his scolding and calmly began eating his dinner. For two or three minutes Neewa kept his hold. Twice he made efforts to pull himself up so that he could get the branch under him. Then his hind feet slipped. For a dozen seconds he hung with his two front paws—then shot down through fifteen feet of space to the ground. Close to Miki he landed with a thud that knocked the wind out of him. He rose with a grunt, took one dazed look up the tree, and without further explanation to Miki began to leg it deeper into the forest—straight into the face of the great adventure which was to be the final test for these two.

VIII

N ot until he had covered at least a quarter of a mile did Neewa stop. To Miki it seemed as though they had come suddenly out of day into the gloom of evening. That part of the forest into which Neewa's flight had led them was like a vast, mysterious cavern. Even Challoner would have paused there, awed by the grandeur of its silence, held spellbound by the enigmatical whispers that made up its only sound. The sun was still high in the heavens, but not a ray of it penetrated the dense green canopy of spruce and balsam that hung like a wall over the heads of Miki and Neewa. About them was no bush, no undergrowth; under their feet was not a flower or a spear of grass. Nothing but a thick, soft carpet of velvety brown needles under which all life was smothered. It was as if the forest nymphs had made of this their bedchamber, sheltered through all the seasons of the year from wind and rain and snow; or else that the were-wolf people—the loup-garou—had chosen it as their hiding-place and from its weird and gloomy fastnesses went forth on their ghostly missions among the sons of men.

Not a bird twittered in the trees. There was no flutter of life in their crowded branches. Everything was so still that Miki heard the excited throbbing of life in his own body. He looked at Neewa, and in the gloom the cub's eyes were glistening with a strange fire. Neither of them was afraid, yet in that cavernous silence their comradeship was born anew, and in it there was something now that crept down into their wild little souls and filled the emptiness that was left by the death of Neewa's mother and the loss of Miki's master. The pup whined gently, and in his throat Neewa made a purring sound and followed it with a squeaky grunt that was like the grunt of a little pig. They edged nearer, and stood shoulder to shoulder facing their world. They went on after a little, like two children exploring the mystery of an old and abandoned house. They were not hunting, yet every hunting instinct in their bodies was awake, and they stopped frequently to peer about them, and listen, and scent the air.

To Neewa it all brought back a memory of the black cavern in which he was born. Would Noozak, his mother, come up presently out of one of those dark forest aisles? Was she sleeping here, as she had slept in the darkness of their den? The questions may have come vaguely in his mind. For it was like the cavern, in that it was deathly still; and a short distance away its gloom thickened into black pits. Such a place the Indians called MUHNEDOO—a spot in the forest blasted of all life by the presence of devils; for only devils would grow trees so thick that sunlight never penetrated. And only owls held the companionship of the evil spirits.

Where Neewa and Miki stood a grown wolf would have paused, and turned back; the fox would have slunk away, hugging the ground; even the murderous-hearted little ermine would have peered in with his beady red eyes, unafraid, but turned by instinct back into the open timber. For here, in spite of the stillness and the gloom, THERE WAS LIFE. It was beating and waiting in the ambush of those black pits. It was rousing itself, even as Neewa and Miki went on deeper into the silence, and eyes that were like round balls were beginning to glow with a greenish fire. Still there was no sound, no movement in the dense overgrowth of the trees. Like the imps of MUHNEDOO the monster owls looked down, gathering their slow wits—and waiting.

And then a huge shadow floated out of the dark chaos and passed so close over the heads of Neewa and Miki that they heard the menacing purr of giant wings. As the wraith-like creature disappeared there came back to them a hiss and the grating snap of a powerful beak. It sent a shiver through Miki. The instinct that had been fighting to rouse itself within him flared up like a powder-flash. Instantly he sensed the nearness of an unknown and appalling danger.

There was sound about them now—movement in the trees, ghostly tremours in the air, and the crackling, metallic SNAP—SNAP—SNAP over their heads. Again Miki saw the great shadow come and go. It was followed by a second, and a third, until the vault under the trees seemed filled with shadows; and with each shadow came nearer that grating menace of powerfully beaked jaws. Like the wolf and the fox he cringed down, hugging the earth. But it was no longer with the whimpering fear of the pup. His muscles were drawn tight, and with a snarl he bared his fangs when one of the owls swooped so low that he felt the beat of its wings. Neewa responded with a sniff that a little later in his life would have been the defiant WHOOF of his mother. Bear-like he was standing up. And it was upon him that one of the shadows descended—a monstrous feathered bolt straight out of darkness.

Six feet away Miki's blazing eyes saw his comrade smothered under a gray mass, and for a moment or two he was held appalled and lifeless by the thunderous beat of the gargantuan wings. No sound came from

Neewa. Flung on his back, he was digging his claws into feathers so thick and soft that they seemed to have no heart or flesh. He felt upon him the presence of the Thing that was death. The beat of the wings was like the beat of clubs: they drove the breath out of his body, they blinded his senses, yet he continued to tear fiercely with his claws into a fleshless breast.

In his first savage swoop Oohoomisew, whose great wings measured five feet from tip to tip, had missed his death-grip by the fraction of an inch. His powerful talons that would have buried themselves like knives in Neewa's vitals closed too soon, and were filled with the cub's thick hair and loose hide. Now he was beating his prey down with his wings until the right moment came for him to finish the killing with the terrific stabbing of his beak. Half a minute of that and Neewa's face would be torn into pieces.

It was the fact that Neewa made no sound, that no cry came from him, that brought Miki to his feet with his lips drawn back and a snarl in his throat. All at once fear went out of him and in its place came a wild and almost joyous exultation. He recognized their enemy—A Bird. To him birds were a prey, and not a menace. A dozen times in their journey down from the Upper Country Challoner had shot big Canada geese and huge-winged cranes. Miki had eaten their flesh. Twice he had pursued wounded cranes, yapping at the top of his voice, And They Had Run From Him. He did not bark or yelp now. Like a flash he launched himself into the feathered mass of the owl. His fourteen pounds of flesh and bone landed with the force of a stone, and Oohoomisew was torn from his hold and flung with a great flutter of wings upon his side.

Before he could recover his balance Miki was at him again, striking full at his head, where he had struck at the wounded crane. Oohoomisew went flat on his back—and for the first time Miki let out of his throat a series of savage and snarling yelps. It was a new sound to Oohoomisew and his blood-thirsty brethren watching the struggle from out of the gloom. The snapping beaks drifted farther away, and Oohoomisew, with a sudden sweep of wings, vaulted into the air.

With his big forefeet planted firmly and his snarling face turned up to the black wall of the tree-tops Miki continued to bark and howl defiantly. He wanted the bird to come back. He wanted to tear and rip at its feathers, and as he sent out his frantic challenge Neewa rolled over, got on his feet, and with a warning squeal to Miki once more set off in flight. If Miki was ignorant in the matter, HE at least understood the situation. Again it was the instinct born of countless generations. He knew that in the black pits about them hovered death—and he ran as he had never run before in his life. As Miki followed, the shadows were beginning to float nearer again.

Ahead of them they saw a glimmer of sunshine. The trees grew taller, and soon the day began breaking through so that there were no longer the cavernous hollows of gloom about them. If they had gone on another hundred yards they would have come to the edge of the big plain, the hunting grounds of the owls. But the flame of self-preservation was hot in Neewa's head; he was still dazed by the thunderous beat of wings; his sides burned where Oohoomisew's talons had scarred his flesh; so, when he saw in his path a tangled windfall of tree trunks he dived into the security of it so swiftly that for a moment or two Miki wondered where he had gone.

Crawling into the windfall after him Miki turned and poked out his head. He was not satisfied. His lips were still drawn back, and he continued to growl. He had beaten his enemy. He had knocked it over fairly, and had filled his jaws with its feathers. In the face of that triumph he sensed the fact that he had run away in following Neewa, and he was possessed with the desire to go back and have it out to a finish. It was the blood of the Airedale and the Spitz growing stronger in him, fearless of defeat; the blood of his father, the giant hunting-hound Hela. It was the demand of his breed, with its mixture of wolfish courage and fox-like persistency backed by the powerful jaws and Herculean strength of the Mackenzie hound, and if Neewa had not drawn deeper under the windfall he would have gone out again and yelped his challenge to the feathered things from which they had fled.

Neewa was smarting under the red-hot stab of Oohoomisew's talons, and he wanted no more of the fight that came out of the air. He began licking his wounds, and after a while Miki went back to him and smelled of the fresh, warm blood. It made him growl. He knew that it was Neewa's blood, and his eyes glowed like twin balls of fire as they watched the opening through which they had entered into the dark tangle of fallen trees.

For an hour he did not move, and in that hour, as in the hour after the killing of the rabbit, he GREW. When at last he crept out cautiously from under the windfall the sun was sinking behind the western forests. He peered about him, watching for movement and listening for sound.

The sagging and apologetic posture of puppyhood was gone from him. His overgrown feet stood squarely on the ground; his angular legs were as hard as if carven out of knotty wood; his body was tense, his ears stood up, his head was rigidly set between the bony shoulders that already gave evidence of gigantic strength to come. About him he knew was the Big Adventure. The world was no longer a world of play and of snuggling under the hands of a master. Something vastly more thrilling had come into it now.

After a time he dropped on his belly close to the opening under the windfall and began chewing at the end of rope which dragged from about his neck. The sun sank lower. It disappeared. Still he waited for Neewa to come out and lie with him in the open. As the twilight thickened into deeper gloom he drew himself into the edge of the door under the windfall and found Neewa there. Together they peered forth into the mysterious night.

For a time there was the utter stillness of the first hour of darkness in the northland. Up in the clear sky the stars came out in twos and then in glowing constellations. There was an early moon. It was already over the edge of the forests, flooding the world with a golden glow, and in that glow the night was filled with grotesque black shadows that had neither movement nor sound. Then the silence was broken. From out of the owl-infested pits came a strange and hollow sound. Miki had heard the shrill screeching and the Tu-Who-O-O, Tu-Who-O-O, Tu-Who-O-O of the little owls, the trap-pirates, but never this voice of the strong-winged Jezebels and Frankensteins of the deeper forests—the real butchers of the night. It was a hollow, throaty sound—more a moan than a cry; a moan so short and low that it seemed born of caution, or of fear that it would frighten possible prey. For a few minutes pit after pit gave forth each its signal of life, and then there was a silence of voice, broken at intervals by the faint, crashing sweep of great wings in the spruce and balsam tops as the hunters launched themselves up and over them in the direction of the plain.

The going forth of the owls was only the beginning of the night carnival for Neewa and Miki. For a long time they lay side by side, sleepless, and listening. Past the windfall went the padded feet of a fisher-cat, and they caught the scent of it; to them came the far cry of a loon, the yapping of a restless fox, and the Mooing of a cow moose feeding in the edge of a lake on the farther side of the plain. And then,

JAMES OLIVER CURWOOD

at last, came the thing that made their blood run faster and sent a deeper thrill into their hearts.

It seemed a vast distance away at first—the hot throated cry of wolves on the trail of meat. It was swinging northward into the plain, and this shortly brought the cry with the wind, which was out of the north and the west. The howling of the pack was very distinct after that, and in Miki's brain nebulous visions and almost unintelligible memories were swiftly wakening into life. It was not Challoner's voice that he heard, but it was A VOICE THAT HE KNEW. It was the voice of Hela, his giant father; the voice of Numa, his mother; the voice of his kind for a hundred and a thousand generations before him, and it was the instinct of those generations and the hazy memory of his earliest puppyhood that were impinging the thing upon him. A little later it would take both intelligence and experience to make him discriminate the hair-breadth difference between wolf and dog. And this voice of his blood was COMING! It bore down upon them swiftly, fierce and filled with the blood-lust of hunger. He forgot Neewa. He did not observe the cub when he slunk back deeper under the windfall. He rose up on his feet and stood stiff and tense, unconscious of all things but that thrilling tongue of the hunt-pack.

Wind-broken, his strength failing him, and his eyes wildly searching the night ahead for the gleam of water that might save him, Ahtik, the young caribou bull, raced for his life a hundred yards ahead of the wolves. The pack had already flung itself out in the form of a horse-shoe, and the two ends were beginning to creep up abreast of Ahtik, ready to close in for the hamstring—and the kill. In these last minutes every throat was silent, and the young bull sensed the beginning of the end. Desperately he turned to the right and plunged into the forest.

Miki heard the crash of his body and he hugged close to the windfall. Ten seconds later Ahtik passed within fifty feet of him, a huge and grotesque form in the moonlight, his coughing breath filled with the agony and hopelessness of approaching death. As swiftly as he had come he was gone, and in his place followed half a score of noiseless shadows passing so quickly that to Miki they were like the coming and the going of the wind.

For many minutes after that he stood and listened but again silence had fallen upon the night. After a little he went back into the windfall and lay down beside Neewa.

Hours that followed he passed in restless snatches of slumber. He dreamed of things that he had forgotten. He dreamed of Challoner. He dreamed of chill nights and the big fires; he heard his master's voice and he felt again the touch of his hand; but over it all and through it all ran that wild hunting voice of his own kind.

In the early dawn he came out from under the windfall and smelled of the trail where the wolves and the caribou had passed. Heretofore it was Neewa who had led in their wandering; now it was Neewa that followed. His nostrils filled with the heavy scent of the pack, Miki travelled steadily in the direction of the plain. It took him half an hour to reach the edge of it. After that he came to a wide and stony outcropping of the earth over which he nosed the spoor to a low and abrupt descent into the wider range of the valley.

Here he stopped.

Twenty feet under him and fifty feet away lay the partly devoured carcass of the young bull. It was not this fact that thrilled him until his heart stood still. From out of the bushy plain had come Maheegun, a renegade she-wolf, to fill herself of the meat which she had not helped to kill. She was a slinking, hollow-backed, quick-fanged creature, still rib-thin from the sickness that had come of eating a poison-bait; a beast shunned by her own kind—a coward, a murderess even of her own whelps. But she was none of these things to Miki. In her he saw in living flesh and bone what his memory and his instinct recalled to him of his mother. And his mother had come before Challoner, his master.

For a minute or two he lay trembling, and then he went down, as he would have gone to Challoner; with great caution, with a wilder suspense, but with a strange yearning within him that the man's presence would have failed to rouse. He was very close to Maheegun before she was conscious that he was near. The Mother-smell was warm in his nose now; it filled him with a great joy; and yet—he was afraid. But it was not a physical fear. Flattened on the ground, with his head between his fore-paws, he whined.

Like a flash the she-wolf turned, her fangs bared the length of her jaws and her bloodshot eyes aglow with menace and suspicion. Miki had no time to make a move or another sound. With the suddenness of a cat the outcast creature was upon him. Her fangs slashed him just once—and she was gone. Her teeth had drawn blood from his shoulder, but it was not the smart of the wound that held him for many moments as still as if dead. The Mother-smell was still where Maheegun had been. But his dreams had crumbled. The thing that had been Memory died away at last in a deep breath that was broken by a whimper of pain. For him, even as for Neewa, there was no more a Challoner, and no longer a mother. But there remained—the world! In it the sun was rising. Out of it came the thrill and the perfume of life. And close to him—very close—was the rich, sweet smell of meat.

He sniffed hungrily. Then he turned, and saw Neewa's black and pudgy body tumbling down the slope of the dip to join him in the feast.

IX

Had Makoki, the leather-faced old Cree runner between God's Lake and Fort Churchill, known the history of Miki and Neewa up to the point where they came to feast on the fat and partly devoured carcass of the young caribou bull, he would have said that Iskoo Wapoo, the Good Spirit of the beasts, was watching over them most carefully. For Makoki had great faith in the forest gods as well as in those of his own tepee. He would have given the story his own picturesque version, and would have told it to the little children of his son's children; and his son's children would have kept it in their memory for their own children later on.

It was not in the ordained nature of things that a black bear cub and a Mackenzie hound pup with a dash of Airedale and Spitz in him should "chum up" together as Neewa and Miki had done. Therefore, he would have said, the Beneficent Spirit who watched over the affairs of four-legged beasts must have had an eye on them from the beginning. It was she—Iskoo Wapoo was a goddess and not a god—who had made Challoner kill Neewa's mother, the big black bear; and it was she who had induced him to tie the pup and the cub together on the same piece of rope, so that when they fell out of the white man's canoe into the rapids they would not die, but would be company and salvation for each other. Neswa-Pawuk ("two little brothers") Makoki would have called them; and had it come to the test he would have cut off a finger before harming either of them. But Makoki knew nothing of their adventures, and on this morning when they came down to the feast he was a hundred miles away, haggling with a white man who wanted a guide. He would never know that Iskoo Wapoo was at his side that very moment, planning the thing that was to mean so much in the lives of Neewa and Miki.

Meanwhile Neewa and Miki went at their breakfast as if starved. They were immensely practical. They did not look back on what had happened, but for the moment submerged themselves completely in the present. The few days of thrill and adventure through which they had gone seemed like a year. Neewa's yearning for his mother had grown less and less insistent, and Miki's lost master counted for nothing now, as things were going with him. Last night was the big, vivid thing in their memories—their fight for life with the monster owls, their flight, the killing of the young caribou bull by the wolves, and (with Miki) the short, bitter experience with Maheegun, the renegade she-wolf. His shoulder burned where she had torn at him with her teeth. But this did not lessen his appetite. Growling as he ate, he filled himself until he could hold no more.

Then he sat back on his haunches and looked in the direction Maheegun had taken.

It was eastward, toward Hudson Bay, over a great plain that lay between two ridges that were like forest walls, yellow and gold in the morning sun. He had never seen the world as it looked to him now. The wolves had overtaken the caribou on a scarp on the high ground that thrust itself out like a short fat thumb from the black and owl-infested forest, and the carcass lay in a meadowy dip that overhung the plain. From the edge of this dip Miki could look down—and so far away that the wonder of what he saw dissolved itself at last into the shimmer of the sun and the blue of the sky. Within his vision lay a paradise of marvellous promise; wide stretches of soft, green meadow; clumps of timber, park-like until they merged into the deeper forest that began with the farther ridge; great patches of bush radiant with the colouring of June; here and there the gleam of water, and half a mile away a lake that was like a giant mirror set in a purplish-green frame of balsam and spruce.

Into these things Maheegun, the she-wolf, had gone. He wondered whether she would come back. He sniffed the air for her. But there was no longer the mother-yearning in his heart. Something had already begun to tell him of the vast difference between the dog and the wolf. For a few moments, still hopeful that the world held a mother for him, he had mistaken her for the one he had lost. But he understood now. A little more and Maheegun's teeth would have snapped his shoulder, or slashed his throat to the jugular. TEBAH-GONE-GAWIN (the One Great Law) was impinging itself upon him, the implacable law of the survival of the fittest. To live was to fight—to kill; to beat everything that had feet or wings. The earth and the air held menace for him. Nowhere, since he had lost Challoner, had he found friendship except in the heart of Neewa, the motherless cub. And he turned toward Neewa now, growling at a gay-plumaged moose-bird that was hovering about for a morsel of meat.

A few minutes before, Neewa had weighed a dozen pounds; now he weighed fourteen or fifteen. His stomach was puffed out like the sides of an overfilled bag, and he sat humped up in a pool of warm sunshine licking his chops and vastly contented with himself and the world. Miki rubbed up to him, and Neewa gave a chummy grunt. Then he rolled over on his fat back and invited Miki to play. It was the first time; and with a joyous yelp Miki jumped into him. Scratching and biting and kicking, and interjecting their friendly scrimmage with ferocious growling on Miki's part and pig-like grunts and squeals on Neewa's, they rolled to the edge of the dip. It was a good hundred feet to the bottom—a steep, grassy slope that ran to the plain—and like two balls they catapulted the length of it. For Neewa it was not so bad. He was round and fat, and went easily.

With Miki it was different. He was all legs and skin and angular bone, and he went down twisting and somersaulting and tying himself into knots until by the time he struck the hard strip of shale at the edge of the plain he was drunk with dizziness and the breath was out of his body. He staggered to his feet with a gasp. For a space the world was whirling round and round in a sickening circle. Then he pulled himself together, and made out Neewa a dozen feet away.

Neewa was just awakening to the truth of an exhilarating discovery. Next to a boy on a sled, or a beaver on its tail, no one enjoys a "slide" more than a black bear cub, and as Miki rearranged his scattered wits Neewa climbed twenty or thirty feet up the slope and deliberately rolled down again! Miki's jaws fell apart in amazement. Again Neewa climbed up and rolled down—and Miki ceased to breathe altogether. Five times he watched Neewa go that twenty or thirty feet up the grassy slope and tumble down. The fifth time he waded into Neewa and gave him a rough-and-tumble that almost ended in a fight.

After that Miki began exploring along the foot of the slope, and for a scant hundred yards Neewa humoured him by following, but beyond that point he flatly refused to go. In the fourth month of his exciting young life Neewa was satisfied that Nature had given him birth that he might have the endless pleasure of filling his stomach. For him, eating was the one and only excuse for existing. In the next few months he had a big job on his hands if he kept up the record of his family, and the fact that Miki was apparently abandoning the fat and juicy carcass of the young bull filled him with alarm and rebellion. Straightway he forgot all thought of play and started back up the slope on a mission that was 100 per cent business.

Observing this, Miki gave up his idea of exploration and joined him.

JAMES OLIVER CURWOOD

They reached the shelf of the dip twenty yards from the carcass of the bull, and from a clutter of big stones looked forth upon their meat. In that moment they stood dumb and paralyzed. Two gigantic owls were tearing at the carcass. To Miki and Neewa these were the monsters of the black forest out of which they had escaped so narrowly with their lives. But as a matter of fact they were not of Oohoomisew's breed of night-seeing pirates. They were Snowy Owls, unlike all others of their kind in that their vision was as keen as a hawk's in the light of broad day. Mispoon, the big male, was immaculately white. His mate, a size or two smaller, was barred with brownish-slate colour—and their heads were round and terrible looking because they had no ear-tufts. Mispoon, with his splendid wings spread half over the carcass of Ahtik, the dead bull, was rending flesh so ravenously with his powerful beak that Neewa and Miki could hear the sound of it. Newish, his mate, had her head almost buried in Ahtik's bowels. The sight of them and the sound of their eating were enough to disturb the nerves of an older bear than Neewa, and he crouched behind a stone, with just his head sticking out.

In Miki's throat was a sullen growl. But he held it back, and flattened himself on the ground. The blood of the giant hunter that was his father rose in him again like fire. The carcass was his meat, and he was ready to fight for it. Besides, had he not whipped the big owl in the forest? But here there were two. The fact held him flattened on his belly a moment or two longer, and in that brief space the unexpected happened.

Slinking up out of the low growth of bush at the far edge of the dip lie saw Maheegun, the renegade she-wolf. Hollow-backed, red-eyed, her bushy tail hanging with the sneaky droop of the murderess, she advanced over the bit of open, a gray and vengeful shadow. Furtive as she was, she at least acted with great swiftness. Straight at Mispoon she launched herself with a snarl and snap of fangs that made Miki hug the ground still closer.

Deep into Mispoon's four-inch armour of feathers Maheegun buried her fangs. Taken at a disadvantage Mispoon's head would have been torn from his body before he could have gathered himself for battle had it not been for Newish. Pulling her blood stained head from Ahtik's flesh and blood she drove at Maheegun with a throaty, wheezing scream—a cry that was like the cry of no other thing that lived. Into the she-wolf's back she sank her beak and talons and Maheegun gave up her grip on Mispoon and tore ferociously at her new assailant. For a space Mispoon was saved, but it was at a terrible sacrifice to Newish. With a single lucky slash of her long-fanged jaws, Maheegun literally tore one of Newish's great wings from her body. The croak of agony that came out of her may have held the death-note for Mispoon, her mate; for he rose on his wings, poised himself for an instant, and launched himself at the she-wolf's back with a force that drove Maheegun off her feet.

Deep into her loins the great owl sank his talons, gripping at the renegade's vitals with an avenging and ferocious tenacity. In that hold Maheegun felt the sting of death. She flung herself on her back; she rolled over and over, snarling and snapping and clawing the air in her efforts to free herself of the burning knives that were sinking still deeper into her bowels. Mispoon hung on, rolling as she rolled, beating with his giant wings, fastening his talons in that clutch that death could not shake loose. On the ground his mate was dying. Her life's blood was pouring out of the hole in her side, but with the dimming vision of death she made a last effort to help Mispoon. And Mispoon, a hero to the last, kept his grip until he was dead.

Into the edge of the bush Maheegun dragged herself. There she freed herself of the big owl. But the deep wounds were still in her sides. The blood dripped from her belly as she made her way down into the thicker cover, leaving a red trail behind her. A quarter of a mile away she lay down under a clump of dwarf spruce; and there, a little later, she died.

To Neewa and Miki—and especially to the son of Hela—the grim combat had widened even more that subtle and growing comprehension of the world as it existed for them. It was the unforgettable wisdom of experience backed by an age-old instinct and the heredity of breed. They had killed small things—Neewa, his bugs and his frogs and his bumble-bees; Miki, his rabbit—they had fought for their lives; they had passed through experiences that, from the beginning, had been a gamble with death; but it had needed the climax of a struggle such as they had seen with their own eyes to open up the doors that gave them a new viewpoint of life.

It was many minutes before Miki went forth and smelled of Newish, the dead owl. He had no desire now to tear at her feathers in the excitement of an infantile triumph and ferocity. Along with greater understanding a new craft and a new cunning were born in him. The fate of Mispoon and his mate had taught him the priceless value of silence and of caution, for he knew now that in the world there were many things that were not afraid of him, and many things that would not run away from him. He had lost his fearless and blatant contempt for winged creatures; he had learned that the earth was not made for him alone, and that to hold his small place on it he must fight as Maheegun and the owls had fought. This was because in Miki's veins was the red fighting blood of a long line of ancestors that reached back to the wolves.

In Neewa the process of deduction was vastly different. His breed was not the fighting breed, except as it fought among its own kind. It did not make a habit of preying upon other beasts, and no other beast preyed upon it. This was purely an accident of birth—the fact that no other creature in all his wide domain was powerful enough, either alone or in groups, to defeat a grown black bear in open battle. Therefore Neewa learned nothing of fighting in the tragedy of Maheegun and the owls. His profit, if any, was in a greater caution. And his chief interest was in the fact that Maheegun and the two owls had not devoured the young bull. His supper was still safe.

With his little round eyes on the alert for fresh trouble he kept himself safely hidden while he watched Miki investigating the scene of battle. From the body of the owl Miki went to Ahtik, and from Ahtik he sniffed slowly over the trail which Maheegun had taken into the bush. In the edge of the cover he found Mispoon. He did not go farther, but returned to Neewa, who by this time had made up his mind that he could safely come out into the open.

Fifty times that day Miki rushed to the defense of their meat. The big-eyed, clucking moose-birds were most annoying. Next to them the Canada jays were most persistent. Twice a little gray-coated ermine, with eyes as red as garnets, came in to get his fill of blood. Miki was at him so fiercely that he did not return a third time. By noon the crows had got scent or sight of the carcass and were circling overhead, waiting for Neewa and Miki to disappear. Later, they set up a raucous protest from the tops of the trees in the edge of the forest.

That night the wolves did not return to the dip. Meat was too plentiful, and those that were over their gorge were off on a fresh kill far to the west. Once or twice Neewa and Miki heard their distant cry.

Again through a star-filled radiant night they watched and listened, and slept at times. In the soft gray dawn they went forth once more to their feast.

And here is where Makoki, the old Cree runner, would have emphasized the presence of the Beneficent Spirit. For day followed day, and night followed night, and Ahtik's flesh and blood put into Neewa and Miki a strength and growth that developed marvellously. By the fourth day Neewa had become so fat and sleek that he was half again as big as on the day he fell out of the canoe. Miki had begun to fill out. His ribs could no longer be counted from a distance. His chest was broadening and his legs were losing some of their angular clumsiness. Practice on Ahtik's bones had strengthened his jaws. With his development he felt less and less the old puppyish desire to play—more and more the restlessness of the hunter. The fourth night he heard again the wailing hunt-cry of the wolves, and it held a wild and thrilling note for him.

With Neewa, fat and good humour and contentment were all synonymous. As long as the meat held out there was no very great temptation for him beyond the dip and the slope. Two or three times a day he went down to the creek; and every morning and afternoon—especially about sunset—he had his fun rolling downhill. In addition to this he began taking his afternoon naps in the crotch of a small sapling. As Miki could see neither sense nor sport in tobogganing, and as he could not climb a tree, he began to spend more and more time in venturing up and down the foot of the ridge. He wanted Neewa to go with him on these expeditions. He never set out until he had entreated Neewa to come down out of his tree, or until he had made an effort to coax him away from the single trail he had made to the creek and back. Neewa's obstinacy would never have brought about any real unpleasantness between them. Miki thought too much of him for that; and if it had come to a final test, and Neewa had thought that Miki would not return, he would undoubtedly have followed him.

It was another and a more potent thing than an ordinary quarrel that placed the first great barrier between them. Now it happened that Miki was of the breed which preferred its meat fresh, while Neewa liked his "well hung." And from the fourth day onward, what was left of Ahtik's carcass was ripening. On the fifth day Miki found the flesh difficult to eat; on the sixth, impossible. To Neewa it became increasingly delectable as the flavour grew and the perfume thickened. On the sixth day, in sheer delight, he rolled in it. That night, for the first time, Miki could not sleep with him.

The seventh day brought the climax. Ahtik now fairly smelled to heaven. The odour of him drifted up and away on the soft June wind until all the crows in the country were gathering. It drove Miki, slinking like a whipped cur, down into the creek bottom. When Neewa came down for a drink after his morning feast Miki sniffed him over for a moment and then slunk away from him again. As a matter of fact, there was small difference between Ahtik and Neewa now, except that one lay still and the other moved. Both smelled dead; both were decidedly "well hung." Even the crows circled over Neewa, wondering why it was that he walked about like a living thing.

That night Miki slept alone under a clump of bush in the creek bottom. He was hungry and lonely, and for the first time in many days he felt the bigness and emptiness of the world. He wanted Neewa. He whined for him in the starry silence of the long hours between sunset and dawn. The sun was well up before Neewa came down the hill. He had finished his breakfast and his morning roll, and he was worse than ever. Again Miki tried to coax him away but Neewa was disgustingly fixed in his determination to remain in his present glory. And this morning he was more than usually anxious to return to the dip. All of yesterday he had found it necessary to frighten the crows away from his meat, and to-day they were doubly persistent in their efforts to rob him. With a grunt and a squeal to Miki he hustled back up the hill after he had taken his drink.

His trail entered the dip through the pile of rocks from which Miki and he had watched the battle between Maheegun and the two owls, and as a matter of caution he always paused for a few moments among these rocks to make sure that all was well in the open. This morning he received a decided shock. Ahtik's carcass was literally black with crows. Kakakew and his Ethiopic horde of scavengers had descended in a cloud, and they were tearing and fighting and beating their wings about Ahtik as if all of them had gone mad. Another cloud was hovering in air; every bush and near-by sapling was bending under the weight of them, and in the sun their jet-black plumage glistened as if they had just come out of the bath of a tinker's pot. Neewa stood astounded. He was not frightened; he had driven the cowardly robbers away many times. But never had there been so many of them. He could see no trace of his meat. Even the ground about it was black.

He rushed out from the rocks with his lips drawn back, just as he had rushed a dozen or more times before. There was a mighty roar of wings. The air was darkened by them, and the ravenish screaming that followed could have been heard a mile away. This time Kakakew and his mighty crew did not fly back to the forest. Their number gave them courage. The taste of Ahtik's flesh and the flavour of it in their nostrils intoxicated them, to the point of madness, with desire. Neewa was dazed. Over him, behind him, on all sides of him they swept and circled, croaking and screaming at him, the boldest of them swooping down to beat at him with their wings. Thicker grew the menacing cloud, and then suddenly it descended like an avalanche. It covered Ahtik again. In it Neewa was fairly smothered. He felt himself buried under a mass of wings and bodies, and he began fighting, as he had fought the owls. A score of pincer-like black beaks fought to get at his hair and hide; others stabbed at his eyes; he felt his ears being pulled from his head, and the end of his nose was a bloody cushion within a dozen seconds. The breath was beaten out of him; he was blinded, and dazed, and every square inch of him was aquiver with its own excruciating pain. He forgot Ahtik. The one thing in the world he wanted most was a large open space in which to run.

Putting all his strength into the effort he struggled to his feet and charged through the mass of living things about him. At this sign of defeat many of the crows left him to join in the feast. By the time he was half way to the cover into which Maheegun had gone all but one had left him. That one may have been Kakakew himself. He had fastened himself like a rat-trap to Neewa's stubby tail, and there he hung on like grim death while Neewa ran. He kept his hold until his victim was well into the cover. Then he flopped himself into the air and rejoined his brethren at the putrified carcass of the bull.

If ever Neewa had wanted Miki he wanted him now. Again his entire viewpoint of the world was changed. He was stabbed in a hundred places. He burned as if afire. Even the bottoms of his feet hurt him when he stepped on them, and for half an hour he hid himself under a bush, licking his wounds and sniffing the air for Miki.

Then he went down the slope into the creek bottom, and hurried to the foot of the trail he had made to and from the dip. Vainly he quested about him for his comrade. He grunted and squealed, and tried to catch the scent of him in the air. He ran up the creek a distance, and back again. Ahtik counted as nothing now.

Miki was gone.

JAMES OLIVER CURWOOD

X

A quarter of a mile away Miki had heard the clamour of the crows. But he was in no humour to turn back, even had he guessed that Neewa was in need of his help. He was hungry from long fasting and, for the present, his disposition had taken a decided turn. He was in a mood to tackle anything in the eating line, no matter how big, but he was a good mile from the dip in the side of the ridge before he found even a crawfish. He crunched this down, shell and all. It helped to take the bad taste out of his mouth.

The day was destined to hold for him still another unforgettable event in his life. Now that he was alone the memory of his master was not so vague as it had been yesterday, and the days before. Brain-pictures came back to him more vividly as the morning lengthened into afternoon, bridging slowly but surely the gulf that Neewa's comradeship had wrought. For a time the exciting thrill of his adventure was gone. Half a dozen times he hesitated on the point of turning back to Neewa. It was hunger that always drove him on a little farther. He found two more crawfish. Then the creek deepened and its water ran slowly, and was darker. Twice he chased old rabbits, that got away from him easily. Once he came within an ace of catching a young one. Frequently a partridge rose with a thunder of wings. He saw moose-birds, and jays, and many squirrels. All about him was meat which it was impossible for him to catch. Then fortune turned his way. Poking his head into the end of a hollow log he cornered a rabbit so completely that there was no escape. During the next few minutes he indulged in the first square meal he had eaten for three days.

So absorbed was he in his feast that he was unconscious of a new arrival on the scene. He did not hear the coming of Oochak, the fisher-cat; nor, for a few moments, did he smell him. It was not in Oochak's nature to make a disturbance. He was by birth and instinct a valiant hunter and a gentleman, and when he saw Miki (whom he took to be a young wolf) feeding on a fresh kill, he made no move to demand a share for himself. Nor did he run away. He would undoubtedly have continued on his way very soon if Miki had not finally sensed his presence, and faced him.

Oochak had come from the other side of the log, and stood not more than six feet distant. To one who knew as little of his history as Miki there was nothing at all ferocious about him. He was shaped like his cousins, the weazel, the mink, and the skunk. He was about half as high as Miki, and fully as long, so that his two pairs of short legs seemed somewhat out of place, as on a dachshund. He probably weighed between eight and ten pounds, had a bullet head, almost no ears, and atrocious whiskers. Also he had a bushy tail and snapping little eyes that seemed to bore clean through whatever he looked at. To Miki his accidental presence was a threat and a challenge. Besides, Oochak looked like an easy victim if it came to a fight. So he pulled back his lips and snarled.

Oochak accepted this as an invitation for him to move on, and being a gentleman who respected other people's preserves he made his apologies by beginning a velvet-footed exit. This was too much for Miki, who had yet to learn the etiquette of the forest trails. Oochak was afraid of him. He was running away! With a triumphant yelp Miki took after him. After all, it was simply a mistake in judgment. (Many two-footed animals with bigger brains than Miki's had made similar mistakes.) For Oochak, attending always to his own business, was, for his size and weight, the greatest little fighter in North America.

Just what happened in the one minute that followed his assault Miki would never be able quite to understand. It was not in reality a fight; it was a one-sided immolation, a massacre. His first impression was that he had tackled a dozen Oochaks instead of one. Beyond that first impression his mind did not work, nor did his eyes visualize. He was whipped as he would never be whipped again in his life. He was cut and bruised and bitten; he was strangled and stabbed; he was so utterly mauled that for a space after Oochak had gone he continued to rake the air with his paws, unconscious of the fact that the affair was over. When he opened his eyes, and found himself alone, he slunk into the hollow log where he had cornered the rabbit.

In there he lay a good half hour, trying hard to comprehend just what had happened. The sun was setting when he dragged himself out. He limped. His one good ear was bitten clean through. There were bare spots on his hide where Oochak had scraped the hair off. His bones ached, his throat was sore, and there was a lump over one eye. He looked longingly back over the "home" trail. Up there was Neewa. With the lengthening shadows of the day's end a great loneliness crept upon him and a desire to turn back to his comrade. But Oochak had gone that way—and he did not want to meet Oochak again.

He wandered a little farther south and east, perhaps a quarter of a mile, before the sun disappeared entirely. In the thickening gloom of twilight he struck the Big Rock portage between the Beaver and the Loon.

It was not a trail. Only at rare intervals did wandering voyageurs coming down from the north make use of it in their passage from one waterway to the other. Three or four times a year at the most would a wolf have caught the scent of man in it. It was there tonight, so fresh that Miki stopped when he came to it as if another Oochak had risen before him. For a space he was turned into the rigidity of rock by a single overwhelming emotion. All other things were forgotten in the fact that he had struck the trail of a man—AND, THEREFORE, THE TRAIL OF CHALLONER, HIS MASTER. He began to follow it—slowly at first, as if fearing that it might get away from him. Darkness came, and he was still following it. In the light of the stars he persisted, all else crowded from him but the homing instinct of the dog and the desire for a master.

At last he came almost to the shore of the Loon, and there he saw the campfire of Makoki and the white man.

He did not rush in. He did not bark or yelp; the hard schooling of the wilderness had already set its mark upon him. He slunk in cautiously— then stopped, flat on his belly, just outside the rim of firelight. Then he saw that neither of the men was Challoner. But both were smoking, as Challoner had smoked. He could hear their voices, and they were like Challoner's voice. And the camp was the same—a fire, a pot hanging over it, a tent, and in the air the odours of recently cooked things.

Another moment or two and he would have gone into the firelight. But the white man rose to his feet, stretched himself as he had often seen Challoner stretch, and picked up a stick of wood as big as his arm. He came within ten feet of Miki, and Miki wormed himself just a little toward him, and stood up on his feet. It brought him into a half light. His eyes were aglow with the reflection of the fire. And the man saw him.

In a flash the club he held was over his head; it swung through the air with the power of a giant arm behind it and was launched straight at Miki. Had it struck squarely it would have killed him. The big end of it missed him; the smaller end landed against his neck and shoulder, driving him back into the gloom with such force and suddenness that the man thought he had done for him. He called out loudly to

Makoki that he had killed a young wolf or a fox, and dashed out into the darkness.

The club had knocked Miki fairly into the heart of a thick ground spruce. There he lay, making no sound, with a terrible pain in his shoulder. Between himself and the fire he saw the man bend over and pick up the club. He saw Makoki hurrying toward him with ANOTHER club, and under his shelter he made himself as small as he could. He was filled with a great dread, for now he understood the truth. THESE men were not Challoner. They were hunting for him—with clubs in their hands. He knew what the clubs meant. His shoulder was almost broken.

He lay very still while the men searched about him. The Indian even poked his stick into the thick ground spruce. The white man kept saying that he was sure he had made a hit, and once he stood so near that Miki's nose almost touched his boot. He went back and added fresh birch to the fire, so that the light of it illumined a greater space about them. Miki's heart stood still. But the men searched farther on, and at last went back to the fire.

For an hour Miki did not move. The fire burned itself low. The old Cree wrapped himself in a blanket, and the white man went into his tent. Not until then did Miki dare to crawl out from under the spruce. With his bruised shoulder making him limp at every step he hurried back over the trail which he had followed so hopefully a little while before. The man-scent no longer made his heart beat swiftly with joy. It was a menace now. A warning. A thing from which he wanted to get away. He would sooner have faced Oochak again, or the owls, than the white man with his club. With the owls he could fight, but in the club he sensed an overwhelming superiority.

The night was very still when he dragged himself back to the hollow log in which he had killed the rabbit. He crawled into it, and nursed his wounds through all the rest of the hours of darkness. In the early morning he came out and ate the rest of the rabbit.

After that he faced the north and west—where Neewa was. There was no hesitation now. He wanted Neewa again. He wanted to muzzle him with his nose and lick his face even though he did smell to heaven. He wanted to hear him grunt and squeal in his funny, companionable way; he wanted to hunt with him again, and play with him, and lie down beside him in a sunny spot and sleep. Neewa, at last, was a necessary part of his world.

JAMES OLIVER CURWOOD

He set out.

And Neewa, far up the creek, still followed hopefully and yearningly over the trail of Miki.

Half way to the dip, in a small open meadow that was a glory of sun, they met. There was no very great demonstration. They stopped and looked at each other for a moment, as if to make sure that there was no mistake. Neewa grunted. Miki wagged his tail. They smelled noses. Neewa responded with a little squeal, and Miki whined. It was as if they had said,

"Hello, Miki!"

"Hello, Neewa!"

And then Neewa lay down in the sun and Miki sprawled himself out beside him. After all, it was a funny world. It went to pieces now and then, but it always came together again. And to-day their world had thoroughly adjusted itself. Once more they were chums—and they were happy.

XI

It was the Flying-Up Moon—deep and slumbering midsummer—in all the land of Keewatin. From Hudson Bay to the Athabasca and from the Hight of Land to the edge of the Great Barrens, forest, plain, and swamp lay in peace and forgetfulness under the sun-glowing days and the star-filled nights of the August Mukoo-Sawin. It was the breeding moon, the growing moon, the moon when all wild life came into its own once more. For the trails of this wilderness world—so vast that it reached a thousand miles east and west and as far north and south—were empty of human life. At the Hudson Bay Company's posts—scattered here and there over the illimitable domain of fang and claw—had gathered the thousands of hunters and trappers, with their wives and children, to sleep and gossip and play through the few weeks of warmth and plenty until the strife and tragedy of another winter began. For these people of the forests it was Mukoo-Sawin—the great Play Day of the year; the weeks in which they ran up new debts and established new credits at the Posts; the weeks in which they foregathered at every Post as at a great fair—playing, and making love, and marrying, and fattening up for the many days of hunger and gloom to come.

It was because of this that the wild things had come fully into the possession of their world for a space. There was no longer the scent of man in all the wilderness. They were not hunted. There were no traps laid for their feet, no poison-baits placed temptingly where they might pass. In the fens and on the lakes the wildfowl squawked and honked unfearing to their young, just learning the power of wing; the lynx played with her kittens without sniffing the air for the menace of man; the cow moose went openly into the cool water of the lakes with their calves; the wolverine and the marten ran playfully over the roofs of deserted shacks and cabins; the beaver and the otter tumbled and frolicked in their dark pools; the birds sang, and through all the wilderness there was the drone and song of Nature as some Great Power must at first have meant that Nature should be. A new generation of wild things had been born. It was a season of Youth, with tens of thousands and hundreds of thousands of little children of the wild playing their first play, learning their first lessons, growing up swiftly to face the menace and doom of their first winter. And the

JAMES OLIVER CURWOOD

Beneficent Spirit of the forests, anticipating what was to come, had prepared well for them. Everywhere there was plenty. The blueberries, the blackberries, the mountain-ash and the saskatoons were ripe; tree and vine were bent low with their burden of fruit. The grass was green and tender from the summer rains. Bulbous roots were fairly popping out of the earth; the fens and the edges of the lakes were rich with things to eat, overhead and underfoot the horn of plenty was emptying itself without stint.

In this world Neewa and Miki found a vast and unending contentment. They lay, on this August afternoon, on a sun-bathed shelf of rock that overlooked a wonderful valley. Neewa, stuffed with luscious blueberries, was asleep. Miki's eyes were only partly closed as he looked down into the soft haze of the valley. Up to him came the rippling music of the stream running between the rocks and over the pebbly bars below, and with it the soft and languorous drone of the valley itself. He napped uneasily for half an hour, and then his eyes opened and he was wide awake. He took a sharp look over the valley. Then he looked at Neewa, who, fat and lazy, would have slept until dark. It was always Miki who kept him on the move. And now Miki barked at him gruffly two or three times, and nipped at one of his ears.

"Wake up!" he might have said. "What's the sense of sleeping on a day like this? Let's go down along the creek and hunt something."

Neewa roused himself, stretched his fat body, and yawned. Sleepily his little eyes took in the valley. Miki got up and gave the low and anxious whine which always told his companion that he wanted to be on the move. Neewa responded, and they began making their way down the green slope into the rich bottom between the two ridges.

They were now almost six months of age, and in the matter of size had nearly ceased to be a cub and a pup. They were almost a dog and a bear. Miki's angular legs were getting their shape; his chest had filled out; his neck had grown until it no longer seemed too small for his big head and jaws, and his body had increased in girth and length until he was twice as big as most ordinary dogs of his age.

Neewa had lost his round, ball-like cubbishness, though he still betrayed far more than Miki the fact that he was not many months lost from his mother. But he was no longer filled with that wholesome love of peace that had filled his earlier cubhood. The blood of Soominitik was at last beginning to assert itself, and he no longer sought a place of safety in time of battle—unless the grimness of utter necessity made it unavoidable. In fact, unlike most bears, he loved a fight. If there were a stronger term at hand it might be applied to Miki, the true son of Hela. Youthful as they were, they were already covered with scars that would have made a veteran proud. Crows and owls, wolf-fang and fisher-claw had all left their marks, and on Miki's side was a bare space eight inches long left as a souvenir by a wolverine.

In Neewa's funny round head there had grown, during the course of events, an ambition to have it out some day with a citizen of his own kind; but the two opportunities that had come his way were spoiled by the fact that the other cubs' mothers were with them. So now, when Miki led off on his trips of adventure, Neewa always followed with another thrill than that of getting something to eat, which so long had been his one ambition. Which is not to say that Neewa had lost his appetite. He could eat more in one day than Miki could eat in three, mainly because Miki was satisfied with two or three meals a day while Neewa preferred one—a continuous one lasting from dawn until dark. On the trail he was always eating something.

A quarter of a mile along the foot of the ridge, in a stony coulee down which a tiny rivulet trickled, there grew the finest wild currants in all the Shamattawa country. Big as cherries, black as ink, and swelling almost to the bursting point with luscious juice, they hung in clusters so thick that Neewa could gather them by the mouthful. Nothing in all the wilderness is quite so good as one of these dead-ripe black currants, and this coulee wherein they grew so richly Neewa had preempted as his own personal property. Miki, too, had learned to eat the currants; so to the coulee they went this afternoon, for such currants as these one can eat even when one is already full. Besides, the coulee was fruitful for Miki in other ways. There were many young partridges and rabbits in it—"fool hens" of tender flesh and delicious flavour which he caught quite easily, and any number of gophers and squirrels.

To-day they had scarcely taken their first mouthful of the big juicy currants when an unmistakable sound came to them. Unmistakable because each recognized instantly what it meant. It was the tearing down of currant bushes twenty or thirty yards higher up the coulee. Some robber had invaded their treasure-house, and instantly Miki bared his fangs while Neewa wrinkled up his nose in an ominous snarl. Soft-footed they advanced toward the sound until they came to the edge of a small open space which was as flat as a table. In the centre of this space was a clump of currant bushes not more than a yard in girth, and black with fruit; and squatted on his haunches there, gathering the laden bushes in his arms, was a young black bear about four sizes larger than Neewa.

In that moment of consternation and rage Neewa did not take size into consideration. He was much in the frame of mind of a man returning home to discover his domicile, and all it contained, in full possession of another. At the same time here was his ambition easily to be achieved—his ambition to lick the daylight out of a member of his own kind. Miki seemed to sense this fact. Under ordinary conditions he would have led in the fray, and before Neewa had fairly got started, would have been at the impudent interloper's throat. But now something held him back, and it was Neewa who first shot out—like a black bolt—landing squarely in the ribs of his unsuspecting enemy.

(Old Makoki, the Cree runner, had he seen that attack, would instantly have found a name for the other bear—"Petoot-a-wapis-kum," which means, literally: "Kicked-off-his-Feet." Perhaps he would have called him "Pete" for short. For the Cree believes in fitting names to fact, and Petoot-a-wapis-kum certainly fitted the unknown bear like a glove.)

Taken utterly by surprise, with his mouth full of berries, he was bowled over like an overfilled bag under the force of Neewa's charge. So complete was his discomfiture for the moment that Miki, watching the affair with a yearning interest, could not keep back an excited yap of approbation. Before Pete could understand what had happened, and while the berries were still oozing from his mouth, Neewa was at his throat—and the fun began.

Now bears, and especially young bears, have a way of fighting that is all their own. It reminds one of a hair-pulling contest between two well-matched ladies. There are no rules to the game—absolutely none. As Pete and Neewa clinched, their hind legs began to do the fighting, and the fur began to fly. Pete, being already on his back—a first-class battling position for a bear—would have possessed an advantage had it not been for Neewa's ferocious hold at his throat. As it was, Neewa sank his fangs in to their full length, and scrubbed away for dear life with his sharp hind claws. Miki drew nearer at sight of the flying fur, his soul filled with joy. Then Pete got one leg into action, and then the other, and Miki's jaws came together with a sudden click. Over and over the two fighters rolled, Neewa holding to his throat-grip, and not a squeal or a grunt came from either of them. Pebbles and dirt flew along with hair and fur. Stones rolled with a clatter down the coulee. The very air trembled with the thrill of combat. In Miki's attitude of tense waiting there was something now of suspicious anxiety. With eight furry legs scratching and tearing furiously, and the two fighters rolling and twisting and contorting themselves like a pair of windmills gone mad, it was almost impossible for Miki to tell who was getting the worst of it—Neewa or Pete; at least he was in doubt for a matter of three or four minutes.

Then he recognized Neewa's voice. It was very faint, but for all that it was an unmistakable bawl of pain.

Smothered under Pete's heavier body Neewa began to realize, at the end of those three or four minutes, that he had tackled more than was good for him. It was altogether Pete's size and not his fighting qualities, for Neewa had him outpointed there. But he fought on, hoping for some good turn of luck, until at last Pete got him just where he wanted him and began raking him up and down his sides until in another three minutes he would have been half skinned if Miki hadn't judged the moment ripe for intervention. Even then Neewa was taking his punishment without a howl.

In another instant Miki had Pete by the ear. It was a grim and terrible hold. Old Soominitik himself would have bawled lustily in the circumstances. Pete raised his voice in a howl of agony. He forgot everything else but the terror and the pain of this new SOMETHING that had him by the ear, and he rent the air with his outcry. His lamentation poured in an unbroken spasm of sound from his throat. Neewa knew that Miki was in action.

He pulled himself from under the young interloper's body—and not a second too soon. Down the coulee, charging like a mad bull, came Pete's mother. Neewa was off like a shot just as she made a powerful swing at him. The blow missed, and the old bear turned excitedly to her bawling offspring. Miki, hanging joyously to his victim, was oblivious of his danger until Pete's mother was almost upon him. He caught sight of her just as her long arm shot out like a wooden beam. He dodged; and the blow intended for him landed full against the side of the unfortunate Pete's head with a force that took him clean off his feet and sent him flying like a football twenty yards down the coulee.

Miki did not wait for further results. Quick as a flash he was in a currant thicket tearing down the little gulch after Neewa. They came out on the plain together, and for a good ten minutes they did not halt

JAMES OLIVER CURWOOD

in their flight long enough to look back. When they did, the coulee was a mile away. They sat down, panting. Neewa's red tongue was hanging out in his exhaustion. He was scratched and bleeding; loose hair hung all over him. As he looked at Miki there was something in the dolorous expression of Neewa's face which was a confession of the fact that he realized Pete had licked him.

XII

After the fight in the coulee there was no longer a thought on the part of Neewa and Miki of returning to the Garden of Eden in which the black currants grew so lusciously. From the tip of his tail to the end of his nose Miki was an adventurer, and like the nomadic rovers of old he was happiest when on the move. The wilderness had claimed him now, body and soul, and it is probable that he would have shunned a human camp at this stage of his life, even as Neewa would have shunned it. But in the lives of beasts, as well as in the lives of men, Fate plays her pranks and tricks, and even as they turned into the vast and mystery-filled spaces of the great lake and waterway-country, to the west, events were slowly shaping themselves into what was to be perhaps the darkest hour of gloom in the life of Miki, son of Hela.

Through six glorious and sun-filled weeks of late summer and early autumn—until the middle of September—Miki and Neewa ranged the country westward, always heading toward the setting sun, the country of Jackson's Knee, of the Touchwood and the Clearwater, and God's Lake. In this country they saw many things. It was a region a hundred miles square which the handiwork of Nature had made into a veritable kingdom of the wild. They came upon great beaver colonies in the dark and silent places; they watched the otter at play; they came upon moose and caribou so frequently that they no longer feared or evaded them, but walked out openly into the meadows or down to the edge of the swamps where they were feeding. It was here that Miki learned the great lesson that claw and fang were made to prey upon cloven hoof and horn, for the wolves were thick, and a dozen times they came upon their kills, and even more frequently heard the wild tongue of the hunting-packs. Since his experience with Maheegun he no longer had the desire to join them. And now Neewa no longer insisted on remaining near meat when they found it. It was the beginning of the KWASKA-HAO in Neewa—the instinctive sensing of the Big Change.

Until early in October Miki could see but little of this change in his comrade. It was then that Neewa became more and more restless, and this restlessness grew as the chill nights came, and autumn breathed more heavily in the air. It was Neewa who took the lead in their peregrinations now, and he seemed always to be questing for something—a mysterious something which Miki could neither smell

JAMES OLIVER CURWOOD

nor see. He no longer slept for hours at a time. By mid-October he slept scarcely at all, but roved through most of the hours of night as well as day, eating, eating, eating, and always smelling the wind for that elusive thing which Nature was commanding him to seek and find. Ceaselessly he was nosing under windfalls and among the rocks, and Miki was always near him, always on the Qui Vive for battle with the thing that Neewa was hunting out. And it seemed to be never found.

Then Neewa turned back to the east, drawn by the instinct of his forefathers; back toward the country of Noozak, his mother, and of Soominitik, his father; and Miki followed. The nights grew more and more chill. The stars seemed farther away, and no longer was the forest moon red like blood. The cry of the loon had a moaning note in it, a note of grief and lamentation. And in their shacks and tepees the forest people sniffed the air of frosty mornings, and soaked their traps in fish-oil and beaver-grease, and made their moccasins, and mended snow-shoe and sledge, for the cry of the loon said that winter was creeping down out of the North. And the swamps grew silent. The cow moose no longer mooed to her young. In place of it, from the open plain and "burn" rose the defiant challenge of bull to bull and the deadly clash of horn against horn under the stars of night. The wolf no longer howled to hear his voice. In the travel of padded feet there came to be a slinking, hunting caution. In all the forest world blood was running red again.

And then—November.

Perhaps Miki would never forget that first day when the snow came. At first he thought all the winged things in the world were shedding their white feathers. Then he felt the fine, soft touch of it under his feet, and the chill. It sent the blood rushing like a new kind of fire through his body; a wild and thrilling joy—the exultation that leaps through the veins of the wolf when the winter comes.

With Neewa its effect was different—so different that even Miki felt the oppression of it, and waited vaguely and anxiously for what was to come. And then, on this day of the first snow, he saw his comrade do a strange and unaccountable thing. He began to eat things that he had never touched as food before. He lapped up soft pine needles, and swallowed them. He ate of the dry, pulpy substance of rotted logs. And then he went into a great cleft broken into the heart of a rocky ridge, and found at last the thing for which he had been seeking. It was a cavern—deep, and dark, and warm.

Nature works in strange ways. She gives to the birds of the air eyes which men may never have, and she gives to the beasts of the earth an instinct which men may never know. For Neewa had come back to sleep his first Long Sleep in the place of his birth—the cavern in which Noozak, his mother, had brought him into the world.

His old bed was still there, the wallow in the soft sand, the blanket of hair Noozak had shed; but the smell of his mother was gone. In the nest where he was born Neewa lay down, and for the last time he grunted softly to Miki. It was as if he felt upon him the touch of a hand, gentle but inevitable, which he could no longer refuse to obey, and to Miki was saying, for the last time: "Good-night!"

That night the Pɪᴘᴏᴏ Kᴇꜱᴛɪɴ—the first storm of winter—came like an avalanche from out of the North. With it came a wind that was like the roaring of a thousand bulls, and over all the land of the wild there was nothing that moved. Even in the depth of the cavern Miki heard the beat and the wail of it and the swishing of the shot-like snow beyond the door through which they had come, and he snuggled close to Neewa, content that they had found shelter.

With the day he went to the slit in the face of the rock, and in his astonishment he made no sound, but stared forth upon a world that was no longer the world he had left last night. Everywhere it was white—a dazzling, eye-blinding white. The sun had risen. It shot a thousand flashing shafts of radiant light into Miki's eyes. So far as his vision could reach the earth was as if covered with a robe of diamonds. From rock and tree and shrub blazed the fire of the sun; it quivered in the tree-tops, bent low with their burden of snow; it was like a sea in the valley, so vivid that the unfrozen stream running through the heart of it was black. Never had Miki seen a day so magnificent. Never had his heart pounded at the sight of the sun as it pounded now, and never had his blood burned with a wilder exultation. He whined, and ran back to Neewa. He barked in the gloom of the cavern and gave his comrade a nudge with his nose. Neewa grunted sleepily. He stretched himself, raised his head for an instant, and then curled himself into a ball again. Vainly Miki protested that it was day, and time for them to be moving. Neewa made no response, and after a while Miki returned to the mouth of the cavern, and looked back to see if Neewa was following him. Then, disappointed, he went out into the snow. For an hour he did not move farther than ten feet away from the den. Three times he returned to Neewa and urged him to get up and come out where it was light. In that far corner of the cavern it was dark, and it was as if he were trying to tell Neewa that he was a dunce to lie there still thinking it was night when the sun was up outside. But he failed. Neewa was in the edge of his Long Sleep—the beginning of Uske-Pow-A-Mew, the dream land of the bears.

Annoyance, the desire almost to sink his teeth in Neewa's ear, gave place slowly to another thing in Miki. The instinct that between beasts is like the spoken reason of men stirred in a strange and disquieting way within him. He became more and more uneasy. There was almost distress in his restlessness as he hovered about the mouth of the cavern. A last time he went to Neewa, and then he started alone down into the valley.

He was hungry, but on this first day after the storm there was small chance of him finding anything to eat. The snowshoe rabbits were completely buried under their windfalls and shelters, and lay quietly in their warm nests. Nothing had moved during the hours of the storm. There were no trails of living things for him to follow, and in places he sank to his shoulders in the soft snow. He made his way to the creek. It was no longer the creek he had known. It was edged with ice. There was something dark and brooding about it now. The sound it made was no longer the rippling song of summer and golden autumn. There was a threat in its gurgling monotone—a new voice, as if a black and forbidding spirit had taken possession of it and was warning him that the times had changed, and that new laws and a new force had come to claim sovereignty in the land of his birth.

He drank of the water cautiously. It was cold—ice-cold. Slowly it was being impinged upon him that in the beauty of this new world that was his there was no longer the warm and pulsing beat of the heart that was life. He was alone. Alone! Everything else was covered up; everything else seemed dead.

He went back to Neewa and lay close to him all through the day. And through the night that followed he did not move again from the cavern. He went only as far as the door and saw celestial spaces ablaze with stars and a moon that rode up into the heavens like a white sun. They, too, seemed no longer like the moon and stars he had known. They were terribly still and cold. And under them the earth was terribly white and silent.

With the coming of dawn he tried once more to awaken Neewa. But this time he was not so insistent. Nor did he have the desire to nip Neewa with his teeth. Something had happened—something which he could not understand. He sensed the thing, but he could not reason it. And he was filled with a strange and foreboding fear.

He went down again to hunt. Under the glory of the moon and stars it had been a wild night of carnival for the rabbits, and in the edge of the timber Miki found the snow beaten hard in places with their tracks. It was not difficult for him to stalk his breakfast this morning. He made his kill, and feasted. He killed again after that, and still again. He could have gone on killing, for now that the snow betrayed them, the hiding-places of the rabbits were so many traps for them. Miki's courage returned. He was fired again with the joy of life. Never had he known such hunting, never had he found such a treasure-house before—not even in the coulee where the currants grew. He ate until he could eat no more, and then he went back to Neewa, carrying with him one of the rabbits he had slain. He dropped it in front of his comrade, and whined. Even then Neewa did not respond, except to draw a deeper breath, and change his position a little.

That afternoon, for the first time in many hours, Neewa rose to his feet, stretched himself, and sniffed of the dead rabbit. But he did not eat. To Miki's consternation he rolled himself round and round in his nest of sand and went to sleep again.

The next day, at about the same time, Neewa roused himself once more. This time he went as far as the mouth of the den, and lapped up a few mouthfuls of snow. But he still refused to eat the rabbit. Again it was Nature telling him that he must not disturb the pine needles and dry bark with which he had padded his stomach and intestines. And he went to sleep again. He did not get up after that.

Day followed day, and, growing lonelier as the winter deepened, Miki hunted alone. All through November he came back each night and slept with Neewa. And Neewa was as if dead, except that his body was warm, and he breathed, and made little sounds now and then in his throat. But this did not satisfy the great yearning that was becoming more and more insistent in Miki's soul, the overwhelming desire for company, for a brotherhood on the trail. He loved Neewa. Through the first long weeks of winter he returned to him faithfully; he brought him meat. He was filled with a strange grief—even greater than if Neewa had been dead. For Miki knew that he was alive, and he could not account for the thing that had happened. Death he would have understood, and FROM death he would have gone away—for good.

JAMES OLIVER CURWOOD

So it came that one night, having hunted far, Miki remained away from the den for the first time, and slept under a deep windfall. After that it was still harder for him to resist the CALL. A second and a third night he went away; and then came the time—inevitable as the coming and going of the moon and stars—when understanding at last broke its way through his hope and his fear, and something told him that Neewa would never again travel with him as through those glorious days of old, when shoulder to shoulder they had faced together the comedies and tragedies of life in a world that was no longer soft and green and warm with a golden sun, but white, and still, and filled with death.

Neewa did not know when Miki went away from the den for the last time. And yet it may be that even in his slumber the Beneficent Spirit may have whispered that Miki was going, for there were restlessness and disquiet in Neewa's dreamland for many days thereafter.

"Be quiet—and sleep!" the Spirit may have whispered. "The Winter is long. The rivers are black and chill, the lakes are covered with floors of ice, and the waterfalls are frozen like great white giants. Sleep! For Miki must go his way, just as the waters of the streams must go their way to the sea. For he is Dog. And you are Bear. SLEEP!"

XIII

In many years there had not been such a storm in all the Northland as that which followed swiftly in the trail of the first snows that had driven Neewa into his den—the late November storm of that year which will long be remembered as KUSKETA PIPPOON (the Black Year), the year of great and sudden cold, of starvation and of death.

It came a week after Miki had left the cavern wherein Neewa was sleeping so soundly. Preceding that, when all the forest world lay under its mantle of white, the sun shone day after day, and the moon and stars were as clear as golden fires in the night skies. The wind was out of the west. The rabbits were so numerous they made hard floors of the snow in thicket and swamp. Caribou and moose were plentiful, and the early cry of wolves on the hunt was like music in the ears of a thousand trappers in shack and teepee.

With appalling suddenness came the unexpected. There was no warning. The day had dawned with a clear sky, and a bright sun followed the dawn. Then the world darkened so swiftly that men on their traplines paused in amazement. With the deepening gloom came a strange moaning, and there was something in that sound that seemed like the rolling of a great drum—the knell of an impending doom. It was THUNDER. The warning was too late. Before men could turn back to safety, or build themselves shelters, the Big Storm was upon them. For three days and three nights it raged like a mad bull from out of the north. In the open barrens no living creature could stand upon its feet. The forests were broken, and all the earth was smothered. All things that breathed buried themselves—or died; for the snow that piled itself up in windrows and mountains was round and hard as leaden shot, and with it came an intense cold.

On the third day it was sixty degrees below zero in the country between the Shamattawa and Jackson's Knee. Not until the fourth day did living things begin to move. Moose and caribou heaved themselves up out of the thick covering of snow that had been their protection; smaller animals dug their way out of the heart of deep drifts and mounds; a half of the rabbits and birds were dead. But the most terrible toll was of men. Many of those who were caught out succeeded in keeping the life within their bodies, and dragged themselves back to teepee and shack. But there were also many who did not return—five

JAMES OLIVER CURWOOD

hundred who died between Hudson Bay and the Athabasca in those three terrible days of the KUSKETA PIPPOON.

In the beginning of the Big Storm Miki found himself in the "burnt" country of Jackson's Knee, and instinct sent him quickly into deeper timber. Here he crawled into a windfall of tangled trunks and tree-tops, and during the three days he did not move. Buried in the heart of the storm, there came upon him an overwhelming desire to return to Neewa's den, and to snuggle up to him once more, even though Neewa lay as if dead. The strange comradeship that had grown up between the two—their wanderings together all through the summer, the joys and hardships of the days and months in which they had fought and feasted like brothers—were memories as vivid in his brain as if it had all happened yesterday. And in the dark wind-fall, buried deeper and deeper under the snow, he dreamed.

He dreamed of Challoner, who had been his master in the days of his joyous puppyhood; he dreamed of the time when Neewa, the motherless cub, was brought into camp, and of the happenings that had come to them afterward; the loss of his master, of their strange and thrilling adventures in the wilderness, and last of all of Neewa's denning-up. He could not understand that. Awake, and listening to the storm, he wondered why it was that Neewa no longer hunted with him, but had curled himself up into a round ball, and slept a sleep from which he could not rouse him. Through the long hours of the three days and nights of storm it was loneliness more than hunger that ate at his vitals. When on the morning of the fourth day he came out from under the windfall his ribs were showing and there was a reddish film over his eyes. First of all he looked south and east, and whined.

Through twenty miles of snow he travelled back that day to the ridge where he had left Neewa. On this fourth day the sun shone like a dazzling fire. It was so bright that the glare of the snow pricked his eyes, and the reddish film grew redder. There was only a cold glow in the west when he came to the end of his journey. Dusk had already begun to settle over the roofs of the forests when he reached the ridge where Neewa had found the cavern. It was no longer a ridge. The wind had piled the snow up over it in grotesque and monstrous shapes. Rocks and bushes were obliterated. Where the mouth of the cavern should have been was a drift ten feet deep. Cold and hungry, thinned by his days and nights of fasting, and with his last hope of comradeship shattered by the pitiless mountains of snow, Miki turned back over his trail. There was nothing left for him now but the old windfall, and his heart was no longer the heart of the joyous comrade and brother of Neewa, the bear. His feet were sore and bleeding, but still he went on. The stars came out; the night was ghostly white in their pale fire; and it was cold—terribly cold. The trees began to snap. Now and then there came a report like a pistol-shot as the frost snapped at the heart of timber. It was thirty degrees below zero. And it was growing colder. With the windfall as his only inspiration Miki drove himself on. Never had he tested his strength or his endurance as he strained them now. Older dogs would have fallen in the trail or have sought shelter or rest. But Miki was the true son of Hela, his giant Mackenzie hound father, and he would have continued until he triumphed—or died.

But a strange thing happened. He had travelled twenty miles to the ridge, and fifteen of the twenty miles back, when a shelf of snow gave way under his feet and he was pitched suddenly downward. When he gathered his dazed wits and stood up on his half frozen legs he found himself in a curious place. He had rolled completely into a wigwam-shaped shelter of spruce boughs and sticks, and strong in his nostrils was the SMELL OF MEAT. He found the meat not more than a foot from the end of his nose. It was a chunk of frozen caribou flesh transfixed on a stick, and without questioning the manner of its presence he gnawed at it ravenously. Only Jacques Le Beau, who lived eight or ten miles to the east, could have explained the situation. Miki had rolled into one of his trap-houses, and it was the bait he was eating.

There was not much of it, but it fired Miki's blood with new life. There was smell in his nostrils now, and he began clawing in the snow. After a little his teeth struck something hard and cold. It was steel—a fisher trap. He dragged it up from under a foot of snow, and with it came a huge rabbit. The snow had so protected the rabbit that, although several days dead, it was not frozen stiff. Not until the last bone of it was gone did Miki's feast end. He even devoured the head. Then he went on to the windfall, and in his warm nest slept until another day.

That day Jacques Le Beau—whom the Indians called "Muchet-ta-aao" (the One with an Evil Heart)—went over his trapline and rebuilt his snow-smothered "houses" and re-set his traps.

It was in the afternoon that Miki, who was hunting, struck his trail in a swamp several miles from the windfall. No longer was his soul stirred by the wild yearning for a master. He sniffed, suspiciously, of Le Beau's snowshoe tracks and the crest along his spine trembled as he caught the wind, and listened. He followed cautiously, and a hundred yards farther on came to one of Le Beau's KEKEKS or trap-shelters. Here too, there was meat—fixed on a peg. Miki reached in. From under his fore-paw came a vicious snap and the steel jaws of a trap flung sticks and snow into his face. He snarled, and for a few moments he waited, with his eyes on the trap. Then he stretched himself until he reached the meat, without advancing his feet. Thus he had discovered the hidden menace of the steel jaws, and instinct told him how to evade them.

For another third of a mile he followed Le Beau's tracks. He sensed the presence of a new and thrilling danger, and yet he did not turn off the trail. An impulse which he was powerless to resist drew him on. He came to a second trap, and this time he robbed the bait-peg without springing the thing which he knew was concealed close under it. His long fangs clicked as he went on. He was eager for a glimpse of the man-beast. But he did not hurry. A third, a fourth, and a fifth trap he robbed of their meat.

Then, as the day ended, he swung westward and covered quickly the five miles between the swamp and his windfall.

Half an hour later Le Beau came back over the line. He saw the first empty KEKEK, and the tracks in the snow.

"TONNERRE!—a wolf!" he exclaimed. "And in broad day!"

Then a slow look of amazement crept into his face, and he fell upon his knees in the snow and examined the tracks.

"NON!" he gasped. "It is a dog! A devil of a wild dog—robbing my traps!"

He rose to his feet, cursing. From the pocket of his coat he drew a small tin box, and from this box he took a round ball of fat. In the heart of the fat was a strychnine capsule. It was a poison-bait, to be set for wolves and foxes.

Le Beau chuckled exultantly as he stuck the deadly lure on the end of the bait-peg.

"Ow, a wild dog," he growled. "I will teach him. To-morrow he will be dead."

On each of the five ravished bait-pegs he placed a strychnine capsule rolled in its inviting little ball of fat.

XIV

T he next morning Miki set out again for the trapline of Jacques Le Beau. It was not the thought of food easily secured that tempted him. There would have been a greater thrill in killing for himself. It was the trail, with its smell of the man-beast, that drew him like a magnet. Where that smell was very strong he wanted to lie down, and wait. Yet with his desire there was also fear, and a steadily growing caution. He did not tamper with the first KEKEK, nor with the second. At the third Le Beau had fumbled in the placing of his bait, and for that reason the little ball of fat was strong with the scent of his hands. A fox would have turned away from it quickly. Miki, however, drew it from the peg and dropped it in the snow between his forefeet. Then he looked about him, and listened for a full minute. After that he licked the ball of fat with his tongue. The scent of Le Beau's hands kept him from swallowing it as he had swallowed the caribou meat. A little suspiciously he crushed it slowly between his jaws. The fat was sweet. He was about to gulp it down when he detected another and less pleasant taste, and what remained in his mouth he spat out upon the snow. But the acrid bite of the poison remained upon his tongue and in his throat. It crept deeper—and he caught up a mouthful of snow and swallowed it to put out the burning sensation that was crawling nearer to his vitals.

Had he devoured the ball of fat as he had eaten the other baits he would have been dead within a quarter of an hour, and Le Beau would not have gone far to find his body. As it was, he was beginning to turn sick at the end of the fifteen minutes. A premonition of the evil that was upon him drew him off the trail and in the direction of the windfall. He had gone only a short distance when suddenly his legs gave way under him, and he fell. He began to shiver. Every muscle in his body trembled. His teeth clicked. His eyes grew wide, and it was impossible for him to move. And then, like a hand throttling him, there came a strange stiffness in the back of his neck, and his breath hissed chokingly out of his throat. The stiffness passed like a wave of fire through his body. Where his muscles had trembled and shivered a moment before they now became rigid and lifeless. The throttling grip of the poison at the base of his brain drew his head back until his muzzle was pointed straight up to the sky. Still he made no cry. For a space every nerve in his body was at the point of death.

JAMES OLIVER CURWOOD

Then came the change. As though a string had snapped, the horrible grip left the back of his neck; the stiffness shot out of his body in a flood of shivering cold, and in another moment he was twisting and tearing up the snow in mad convulsions. The spasm lasted for perhaps a minute. When it was over Miki was panting. Streams of saliva dripped from his jaws into the snow. But he was alive. Death had missed him by a hair, and after a little he staggered to his feet and continued on his way to the windfall.

Thereafter Jacques Le Beau might place a million poison capsules in his way and he would not touch them. Never again would he steal the meat from a bait-peg.

Two days later Le Beau saw where Miki had fought his fight with death in the snow and his heart was black with rage and disappointment. He began to follow the footprints of the dog. It was noon when he came to the windfall and saw the beaten path where Miki entered it. On his knees he peered into the cavernous depths—and saw nothing. But Miki, lying watchfully, saw the man, and he was like the black, bearded monster who had almost killed him with a club a long time ago. And in his heart, too, there was disappointment, for away back in his memory of things there was always the thought of Challoner—the master he had lost; and it was never Challoner whom he found when he came upon the man smell.

Le Beau heard his growl, and the man's blood leapt excitedly as he rose to his feet. He could not go in after the wild dog, and he could not lure him out. But there was another way. He would drive him out with fire!

Deep back in his fortress, Miki heard the crunch of Le Beau's feet in the snow. A few minutes later he saw the man-beast again peering into his lair.

"Bete, Bete," he called half tauntingly, and again Miki growled.

Jacques was satisfied. The windfall was not more than thirty or forty feet in diameter, and about it the forest was open and clear of undergrowth. It would be impossible for the wild dog to get away from his rifle.

A second time he went around the piled-up mass of fallen timber. On three sides it was completely smothered under the deep snow. Only where Miki's trail entered was it open.

Getting the wind behind him Le Beau made his Iskoo of birch-bark and dry wood at the far end of the windfall. The seasoned logs and tree-tops caught the fire like tinder, and within a few minutes the flames began to crackle and roar in a manner that made Miki wonder what was happening. For a space the smoke did not reach him. Le Beau, watching, with his rifle in his bare hands, did not for an instant let his eyes leave the spot where the wild dog must come out.

Suddenly a pungent whiff of smoke filled Miki's nostrils, and a thin white cloud crept in a ghostly veil between him and the opening. A crawling, snake-like rope of it began to pour between two logs within a yard of him, and with it the strange roaring grew nearer and more menacing. Then, for the first time, he saw lightning flashes of yellow flame through the tangled debris as the fire ate into the heart of a mass of pitch-filled spruce. In another ten seconds the flames leapt twenty feet into the air, and Jacques Le Beau stood with his rifle half to his shoulder, ready to kill.

Appalled by the danger that was upon him, Miki did not forget Le Beau. With an instinct sharpened to fox-like keenness his mind leapt instantly to the truth of the matter. It was the man-beast who had set this new enemy upon him; and out there, just beyond the opening, the man-beast was waiting. So, like the fox, he did what Le Beau least expected. He crawled back swiftly through the tangled tops until he came to the wall of snow that shut the windfall in, and through this he burrowed his way almost as quickly as the fox himself would have done it. With his jaws he tore through the half-inch outer crust, and a moment later stood in the open, with the fire between him and Le Beau.

The windfall was a blazing furnace, and suddenly Le Beau ran back a dozen steps so that he could see on the farther side. A hundred yards away he saw Miki making for the deeper forest.

It was a clear shot. At that distance Le Beau would have staked his life that it was impossible for him to miss. He did not hurry. One shot, and it would be over. He raised his rifle, and in that instant a wisp of smoke came like the lash of a whip with the wind and caught him fairly in the eyes, and his bullet passed three inches over Miki's head. The whining snarl of it was a new thing to Miki. But he recognized the thunder of the gun—and he knew what a gun could do. To Le Beau, still firing at him through the merciful cloud of smoke, he was like a gray streak flashing to the thick timber. Three times more Le Beau fired. From the edge of a dense clump of spruce Miki flung back a defiant howl. He disappeared as Le Beau's last shot shovelled up the snow at his heels.

JAMES OLIVER CURWOOD

The narrowness of his escape from the man-beast did not frighten Miki out of the Jackson's Knee country. If anything, it held him more closely to it. It gave him something to think about besides Neewa and his aloneness. As the fox returns to peer stealthily upon the deadfall that has almost caught him, so the trapline was possessed now of a new thrill for Miki. Heretofore the man-smell had held for him only a vague significance; now it marked the presence of a real and concrete danger. And he welcomed it. His wits were sharpened. The fascination of the trapline was deadlier than before.

From the burned windfall he made a wide detour to a point where Le Beau's snowshoe trail entered the edge of the swamp; and here, hidden in a thick clump of bushes, he watched him as he travelled homeward half an hour later.

From that day he hung like a grim, gray ghost to the trapline. Silent-footed, cautious, always on the alert for the danger which threatened him, he haunted Jacques Le Beau's thoughts and footsteps with the elusive persistence of a were-wolf—a loup-garou of the Black Forest. Twice in the next week Le Beau caught a flash of him. Three times he heard him howl. And twice he followed his trail until, in despair and exhaustion, he turned back. Never was Miki caught unaware. He ate no more baits in the trap-houses. Even when Le Beau lured him with the whole carcass of a rabbit he would not touch it, nor would he touch a rabbit frozen dead in a snare. From Le Beau's traps he took only the living things, chiefly birds and squirrels and the big web-footed snowshoe rabbits. And because a mink jumped at him once, and tore open his nose, he destroyed a number of minks so utterly that their pelts were spoiled. He found himself another windfall, but instinct taught him now never to go to it directly, but to approach it, and leave it, in a roundabout way.

Day and night Le Beau, the man-brute, plotted against him. He set many poison-baits. He killed a doe, and scattered strychnine in its entrails. He built deadfalls, and baited them with meat soaked in boiling fat. He made himself a "blind" of spruce and cedar boughs, and sat for long hours, watching with his rifle. And still Miki was the victor.

One day Miki found a huge fisher-cat in one of the traps. He had not forgotten the battle of long ago with Oochak, the other fisher-cat, or the whipping he had received. But there was no thought of vengeance in his heart on the early evening he became acquainted with Oochak the Second. Usually he was in his windfall at dusk, but this afternoon a great and devouring loneliness had held him on the trail. The spirit of Kuskayetum—the hand of the mating-god—was pressing heavily upon him; the consuming desire of flesh and blood for the companionship of other flesh and blood. It burned in his veins like a fever. It took away from him all thought of hunger or of the hunt. In his soul was a vast, unfilled yearning.

It was then that he came upon Oochak. Perhaps it was the same Oochak of months ago. If so, he had grown even as Miki had grown. He was splendid, with his long silken fur and his sleek body, and he was not struggling, but sat awaiting his fate without excitement. To Miki he looked warm and soft and comfortable. It made him think of Neewa, and the hundred and one nights they had slept together. His desire leapt out to Oochak. He whined softly as he advanced. He would make friends. Even with Oochak, his old enemy, he would lie down in peace and happiness, so great was the gnawing emptiness in his heart.

Oochak made no response, nor did he move, but sat furred up like a huge soft ball, watching Miki as he crept nearer on his belly. Something of the old puppishness came back into the dog. He wriggled and thumped his tail, and as he whined again he seemed to say.

"Let's forget the old trouble, Oochak. Let's be friends. I've got a fine windfall—and I'll kill you a rabbit."

And still Oochak did not move or make a sound. At last Miki could almost reach out with his forepaws and touch him. He dragged himself still nearer, and his tail thumped harder.

"And I'll get you out of the trap," he may have been saying. "It's the man-beast's trap—and I hate him."

And then, so suddenly that Miki had no chance to guard himself, Oochak sprang the length of the trap-chain and was at him. With teeth and razor-edged claws he tore deep gashes in Miki's nose. Even then the blood of battle rose slowly in him, and he might have retreated had not Oochak's teeth got a hold in his shoulder. With a roar he tried to shake himself free, but Oochak held on. Then his jaws snapped at the back of the fisher-cat's neck. When he was done Oochak was dead.

He slunk away, but in him there was no more the thrill of the victor. He had killed, but in killing he had found no joy. Upon him—the four-footed beast—had fallen at last the oppression of the thing that drives men mad. He stood in the heart of a vast world, and for him that world was empty. He was an outcast. His heart crying out for comradeship, he found that all things feared him or hated him. He was a pariah; a

JAMES OLIVER CURWOOD

wanderer without a friend or a home. He did not reason these things but the gloom of them settled upon him like black night.

He did not return to his windfall. In a little open he sat on his haunches, listening to the night sounds, and watching the stars as they came out. There was an early moon, and as it came up over the forest, a great throbbing red disc that seemed filled with life, he howled mournfully in the face of it. He wandered out into a big burn a little later, and there the night was like day, so clear that his shadow followed him and all other things about him cast shadows, And then, all at once, he caught in the night wind a sound which he had heard many times before.

It came from far away, and it was like a whisper at first, an echo of strange voices riding on the wind, A hundred times he had heard that cry of the wolves. Since Maheegun, the she-wolf, had gashed his shoulder so fiercely away back in the days of his puppyhood he had evaded the path of that cry. He had learned, in a way, to hate it. But he could not wipe out entirely the thrill that came with that call of the blood. And to-night it rode over all his fear and hatred. Out there was COMPANY. Whence the cry came the wild brethren were running two by two, and three by three, and there was COMRADESHIP. His body quivered. An answering cry rose in his throat, dying away in a whine, and for an hour after that he heard no more of the wolf-cry in the wind. The pack had swung to the west— so far away that their voices were lost. And it passed—with the moon straight over them—close to the shack of Pierrot, the halfbreed.

In Pierrot's cabin was a white man, on his way to Fort O' God. He saw that Pierrot crossed himself, and muttered.

"It is the mad pack," explained Pierrot then. "M'sieu, they have been KESKWAO since the beginning of the new moon. In them are the spirits of devils."

He opened the cabin door a little, so that the mad cry of the beasts came to them plainly. When he closed it there was in his eyes a look of strange fear.

"Now and then wolves go like that—KESKWAO (stark mad)—in the dead of winter," he shuddered. "Three days ago there were twenty of them, m'sieu, for I saw them with my own eyes, and counted their tracks in the snow. Since then they been murdered and torn into strings by the others of the pack. Listen to them ravin'! Can you tell me why, m'sieu? Can you tell me why wolves sometimes go mad in the heart of winter when there is no heat or rotten meat to turn them sick? NON? But I can tell you. They are the loups-garous; in their bodies ride the spirits of devils, and there they will ride until the bodies die. For the wolves that go mad in the deep snows always die, m'sieu. That is the strange part of it. THEY DIE!"

And then it was, swinging eastward from the cabin of Pierrot, that the mad wolves of Jackson's Knee came into the country of the big swamp wherein trees bore the Double-X blaze of Jacques Le Beau's axe. There were fourteen of them running in the moonlight. What it is that now and then drives a wolf-pack mad in the dead of winter no man yet has wholly learned. Possibly it begins with a "bad" wolf; just as a "bad" sledge-dog, nipping and biting his fellows, will spread his distemper among them until the team becomes an ugly, quarrelsome horde. Such a dog the wise driver kills—or turns loose.

The wolves that bore down upon Le Beau's country were red-eyed and thin. Their bodies were covered with gashes, and the mouths of some frothed blood. They did not run as wolves run for meat. They were a sinister and suspicious lot, with a sneaking droop to their haunches, and their cry was not the deep-throated cry of the hunt-pack but a ravening clamour that seemed to have no leadership or cause. Scarcely was the sound of their tongues gone beyond the hearing of Pierrot's ears than one of the thin gray beasts rubbed against the shoulder of another, and the second turned with the swiftness of a snake, like the "bad" dog of the traces, and struck his fangs deep into the first wolf's flesh. Could Pierrot have seen, he would have understood then how the four he had found had come to their end.

Swift as the snap of a whip-lash the fight between the two was on. The other twelve of the pack stopped. They came back, circling in cautiously and grimly silent about their fighting comrades. They ranged themselves in a ring, as men gather about a fistic battle; and there they waited, their jaws drooling, their fangs clicking, a low and eager whining smothered in their throats. And then the thing happened. One of the fighting wolves went down. He was on his back—and the end came. The twelve wolves were upon him as one, and, like those Pierrot had seen, he was torn to pieces, and his flesh devoured. After that the thirteen went on deeper into Le Beau's country.

Miki heard them again, after that hour's interval of silence. Farther and farther he had wandered from the forest. He had crossed the "burn," and was in the open plain, with the rough ridges cutting through and the big river at the edge of it. It was not so gloomy out

JAMES OLIVER CURWOOD

here, and his loneliness weighed upon him less heavily than in the deep timber.

And across this plain came the voice of the wolves.

He did not move away from it to-night. He waited, silhouetted against the vivid starlight at the crest of a rocky knoll, and the top of this knoll was so small that another could not have stood beside him without their shoulders touching. On all sides of him the plain swept away in the white light of the stars and moon; never had the desire to respond to the wild brethren urged itself upon him more fiercely than now. He flung back his head, until his black-tipped muzzle pointed up to the stars, and the voice rolled out of his throat. But it was only half a howl. Even then, oppressed by his great loneliness, there gripped him that something instinctive which warned him against betrayal. After that he remained quiet, and as the wolves drew nearer his body grew tense, his muscles hardened, and in his throat there was the low whispering of a snarl instead of a howl. He sensed danger. He had caught, in the voice of the wolves, the ravening note that had made Pierrot cross himself and mutter of the loups-garous, and he crouched down on his belly at the top of the rocky mound.

Then he saw them. They were sweeping like dark and swiftly moving shadows between him and the forest. Suddenly they stopped, and for a few moments no sound came from them as they packed themselves closely on the scent of his fresh trail in the snow. And then they surged in his direction; this time there was a still fiercer madness in the wild cry that rose from their throats. In a dozen seconds they were at the mound. They swept around it and past it, all save one—a huge gray brute who shot up the hillock straight at the prey the others had not yet seen. There was a snarl in Miki's throat as he came. Once more he was facing the thrill of a great fight. Once more the blood ran suddenly hot in his veins, and fear was driven from him as the wind drives smoke from a fire. If Neewa were only there now, to fend at his back while he fought in front! He stood up on his feet. He met the up-rushing pack-brute head to head. Their jaws clashed, and the wild wolf found jaws at last that crunched through his own as if they had been whelp's bone, and he rolled and twisted back to the plain in a dying agony. But not until another gray form had come to fill his place. Into the throat of this second Miki drove his fangs as the wolf came over the crest. It was the slashing, sabre-like stroke of the north-dog, and the throat of the wolf was torn open and the blood poured out as if emptied by the blade of a knife. Down he plunged to join the first, and in that instant the pack swept up and over Miki, and he was smothered under the mass of their bodies. Had two or three attacked him at once he would have died as quickly as the first two of his enemies had come to their end. Numbers saved him in the first rush. On the level of the plain he would have been torn into pieces like a bit of cloth, but on the space at the top of the KOPJE, no larger than the top of a table, he was lost for a few seconds under the snarling and rending horde of his enemies. Fangs intended for him sank into other wolf-flesh; the madness of the pack became a blind rage, and the assault upon Miki turned into a slaughter of the wolves themselves. On his back, held down by the weight of bodies, Miki drove his fangs again and again into flesh. A pair of jaws seized him in the groin, and a shock of agony swept through him. It was a death-grip, sinking steadily into his vitals. Just in time another pair of jaws seized the wolf who held him, and the hold in his groin gave way. In that moment Miki felt himself plunging down the steep side of the knoll, and after him came a half of what was left alive of the pack.

The fighting devils in Miki's brain gave way all at once to that cunning of the fox which had served him even more than claw and fang in times of great danger. Scarcely had he reached the plain before he was on his feet, and no sooner had he touched his feet than he was off like the wind in direction of the river. He had gained a fifty-yard start before the first of the wolves discovered his flight. There were only eight that followed him now. Of the thirteen mad beasts five were dead or dying at the foot of the hillock. Of these Miki had slain two. The others had fallen at the fangs of their own brethren.

Half a mile away were the steep cliffs of the river, and at the edge of these cliffs was a great cairn of rocks in which for one night Miki had sought shelter. He had not forgotten the tunnel into the tumbled mass of rock debris, nor how easily it could be defended from within. Once in that tunnel he would turn in the door of it and slaughter his enemies one by one, for only one by one could they attack him. But he had not reckoned with that huge gray form behind him that might have been named Lightning, the fiercest and swiftest of all the mad wolves of the pack. He sped ahead of his slower-footed companions like a streak of light, and Miki had made but half the distance to the cairn when he heard the panting breath of Lightning behind him. Even Hela, his father, could not have run more swiftly than Miki, but great as was Miki's speed, Lightning ran more swiftly. Two thirds of the distance to the cliff and the huge wolf's muzzle was at Miki's flank. With a burst of speed Miki gained a little. Then steadily Lightning drew abreast of him, a grim and merciless shadow of doom.

A hundred yards farther on and a little to the right was the cairn. But Miki could not run to the right without turning into Lightning's jaws, and he realized now that if he reached the cairn his enemy would be upon him before he could dive into the tunnel and face about. To stop and fight would be death, for behind he could hear the other wolves. Ten seconds more and the chasm of the river yawned ahead of them.

At its very brink Miki swung and struck at Lightning. He sensed death now, and in the face of death all his hatred turned upon the one beast that had run at his side. In an instant they were down. Two yards from the edge of the cliff, and Miki's jaws were at Lightning's throat when the pack rushed upon them. They were swept onward. The earth flew out from under their feet, and they were in space. Grimly Miki held to the throat of his foe. Over and over they twisted in mid-air, and then came a terrific shock. Lightning was under. Yet so great was the shock, that, even though the wolf's huge body was under him like a cushion, Miki was stunned and dazed. A minute passed before he staggered to his feet. Lightning lay still, the life smashed out of him. A little beyond him lay the bodies of two other wolves that in their wild rush had swept over the cliff.

Miki looked up. Between him and the stars he could see the top of the cliff, a vast distance above him. One after the other he smelled at the bodies of the three dead wolves. Then he limped slowly along the base of the cliff until he came to a fissure between two huge rocks. Into this he crept and lay down, licking his wounds. After all there were worse things in the world than Le Beau's trapline. Perhaps there were even worse things than men.

After a time he stretched his great head out between his fore-paws, and slowly the starlight grew dimmer, and the snow less white, and he slept.

XV

In a twist of Three Jackpine River, buried in the deep of the forest between the Shamattawa country and Hudson Bay, was the cabin in which lived Jacques Le Beau, the trapper. There was not another man in all that wilderness who was the equal of Le Beau in wickedness—unless it was Durant, who hunted foxes a hundred miles north, and who was Jacques's rival in several things. A giant in size, with a heavy, sullen face and eyes which seemed but half-hidden greenish loopholes for the pitiless soul within him—if he had a soul at all—Le Beau was a "throw-back" of the worst sort. In their shacks and teepees the Indians whispered softly that all the devils of his forebears had gathered in him.

It was a grim kind of fate that had given to Le Beau a wife. Had she been a witch, an evil-doer and an evil-thinker like himself, the thing would not have been such an abortion of what should have been. But she was not that. Sweet-faced, with something of unusual beauty still in her pale cheeks and starving eyes—trembling at his approach and a slave in his presence—she was, like his dogs, the PROPERTY of The Brute. And the woman had a baby. One had already died; and it was the thought that this one might die, as the other had died, that brought at times the new flash of fire into her dark eyes.

"Le bon Dieu—I pray to the Blessed Angels—I swear you SHALL live!" she would cry to it at times, hugging it close to her breast. And it was at these times that the fire came into her eyes, and her pale cheeks flushed with a smouldering bit of the flame that had once been her beauty. "Some day—SOME DAY—"

But she never finished, even to the child, what was in her mind. Sometimes her dreams were filled with visions. The world was still young, and SHE was not old. She was thinking of that as she stood before the cracked bit of mirror in the cabin, brushing out her hair, that was black and shining and so long that it fell to her hips. Of her beauty her hair had remained. It was defiant of The Brute. And deep back in her eyes, and in her face, there were still the living, hidden traces of her girlhood heritage ready to bloom again if Fate, mending its error at last, would only take away forever the crushing presence of the Master. She stood a little longer before the bit of glass when she heard the crunching of footsteps in the snow outside.

JAMES OLIVER CURWOOD

Swiftly what had been in her face was gone. Le Beau had been away on his trapline since yesterday, and his return filled her with the old dread. Twice he had caught her before the mirror and had called her vile names for wasting her time in admiring herself when she might have been scraping the fat from his pelts. The second time he had sent her reeling back against the wall, and had broken the mirror until the bit she treasured now was not much larger than her two slim hands. She would not be caught again. She ran with the glass to the place where she kept it in hiding, and then quickly she wove the heavy strands of her hair into a braid. The strange, dead look of fear and foreboding closed like a veil over the secrets her eyes had disclosed to herself. She turned, as she always turned in her woman's hope and yearning, to greet him when he entered.

The Brute entered, a dark and surly monster. He was in a wicked humour. His freshly caught furs he flung to the floor. He pointed to them, and his eyes were narrowed to menacing slits as they fell upon her.

"He was there again—that devil!" he growled. "See, he has spoiled the fisher, and he has cleaned out my baits and knocked down the trap-houses. Par les mille cornes du diable, but I will kill him! I have sworn to cut him into bits with a knife when I catch him—and catch him I will, to-morrow. See to it there—the skins—when you have got me something to eat. Mend the fisher where he is torn in two, and cover the seam well with fat so that the agent over at the post will not discover it is bad. Tonnerre de Dieu!—that brat! Why do you always keep his squalling until I come in? Answer me, Bete!"

Such was his greeting. He flung his snowshoes into a corner, stamped the snow off his feet, and got himself a fresh plug of black tobacco from a shelf over the stove. Then he went out again, leaving the woman with a cold tremble in her heart and the wan desolation of hopelessness in her face as she set about getting him food.

From the cabin Le Beau went to his dog-pit, a corral of saplings with a shelter-shack in the centre of it. It was The Brute's boast that he had the fiercest pack of sledge-dogs between Hudson Bay and the Athabasca. It was his chief quarrel with Durant, his rival farther north; and his ambition was to breed a pup that would kill the fighting husky which Durant brought down to the Post with him each winter at New Year. This season he had chosen Netah ("The Killer") for the big fight at God's Lake. On the day he would gamble his money and his reputation against Durant's, his dog would be just one month under two years of age. It was Netah he called from out of the pack now.

The dog slunk to him with a low growl in his throat, and for the first time something like joy shone in Le Beau's face. He loved to hear that growl. He loved to see the red and treacherous glow in Netah's eyes, and hear the menacing click of his jaws. Whatever of nobility might have been in Netah's blood had been clubbed out by the man. They were alike, in that their souls were dead. And Netah, for a dog, was a devil. For that reason Le Beau had chosen him to fight the big fight.

Le Beau looked down at him, and drew a deep breath of satisfaction.

"Ow! but you are looking fine, Netah," he exulted. "I can almost see running blood in those devil-eyes of yours; Oui—red blood that smells and runs, as the blood of Durant's Poos shall run when you sink those teeth in its jugular. And to-morrow we are going to give you the test—such a beautiful test!—with the wild dog that is robbing my traps and tearing my fishers into bits. For I will catch him, and you shall fight him until he is almost dead; and then I shall cut his heart out alive, as I have promised, and you will eat it while it is still beating, so that there will be no excuse for your losing to that Poos which M'sieu Durant will bring down. Comprenez? It will be a beautiful test—to-morrow. And if you fail I will kill you. Oui; if you so much as let a whimper out of you, I will kill you—dead."

XVI

That same night, ten miles to the west, Miki slept under a windfall of logs and treetops not more than half a mile from Le Beau's trapline.

In the early dawn, when Le Beau left his cabin, accompanied by Netah, The Killer, Miki came out from under his windfall after a night of troublous dreams. He had dreamed of those first weeks after he had lost his master, when Neewa was always at his side; and the visions that had come to him filled him with an uneasiness and a loneliness that made him whine as he stood watching the dark shadows fading away before the coming of day. Could Le Beau have seen him there, as the first of the cold sun struck upon him, the words which he had repeated over and over to The Killer would have stuck in his throat. For at eleven months of age Miki was a young giant of his breed. He weighed sixty pounds, and none of that sixty was fat. His body was as slim and as lean as a wolf's. His chest was massive, and over it the muscles rolled like BABICHE cord when he moved. His legs were like the legs of Hela, the big Mackenzie hound who was his father; and with his jaws he could crack a caribou bone as Le Beau might have cracked it with a stone. For eight of the eleven months of his life the wilderness had been his master; it had tempered him to the hardness of living steel; it had wrought him without abeyance to age in the mould of its pitiless schooling—had taught him to fight for his life, to kill that he might live, and to use his brain before he used his jaws. He was as powerful as Netah, The Killer, who was twice his age, and with his strength he possessed a cunning and a quickness which The Killer would never know. Thus had the raw wilderness prepared him for this day.

As the sun fired up the forest with a cold flame Miki set off in direction of Le Beau's trapline. He came to where Le Beau had passed yesterday and sniffed suspiciously of the man-smell that was still strong in the snowshoe tracks. He had become accustomed to this smell, but he had not lost his suspicion of it. It was repugnant to him, even as it fascinated him. It filled him with an inexplicable fear, and yet he found himself powerless to run away from it. Three times in the last ten days he had seen the man-brute himself. Once he had been hiding within a dozen yards of Le Beau when he passed.

This morning he headed straight for the swamp through which Le Beau's traps were set. There the rabbits were thickest and it was in the swamp that they most frequently got in Jacques's KEKEKS—the little houses he built of sticks and cedar boughs to keep the snow off his baits. They were so numerous that they were a pest, and each time that Le Beau made his trip over the line he found at least two out of every three traps sprung by them, and therefore made useless for the catching of fur. But, where there were many rabbits there were also fishers and lynx, and in spite of the rage which the plague of rabbits sent him into, Le Beau continued to set his traps there. And now, in addition to the rabbits, he had the wild dog to contend with.

His heart was fired by a vengeful anticipation as he hurried on through the glow of the early sun, with The Killer at his heels, led by a BABICHE thong. Miki was nosing about the first trap-house as Netah and Le Beau entered the edge of the swamp, three miles to the east.

It was in this KEKEK that Miki had killed the fisher-cat the previous morning. It was empty now. Even the bait-peg was gone, and there was no sign of a trap. A quarter of a mile farther on he came to a second trap-house, and this also was empty. He was a bit puzzled. And then he went on to the third house. He stood for several minutes, sniffing the air still more suspiciously, before he drew close to it. The man-tracks were thicker here. The snow was beaten down with them, and the scent of Le Beau was so strong in the air that for a space Miki believed he was near. Then he advanced so that he got a look into the door of the trap-house. Squatted there, staring at him with big round eyes, was a huge snowshoe rabbit. A premonition of danger held Miki back. It was something in the attitude of Wapoos, the old rabbit. He was not like the others he had caught along Le Beau's line. He was not struggling in a trap; he was not stretched out, half frozen, and he was not dangling at the end of a snare. He was all furred up into a warm and comfortable looking ball. As a matter of fact, Le Beau had caught him with his hands in a hollow log, and had tied him to the bait peg with a piece of buck-skin string; and after that, just out of Wapoos's reach, he had set a nest of traps and covered them with snow.

Nearer and nearer to this menace drew Miki, in spite of the unaccountable impulse that warned him to keep back. Wapoos, fascinated by his slow and deadly advance, made no movement, but sat as if frozen into stone. Then Miki was at him. His powerful jaws closed with a crunch. In the same instant there came the angry snap of steel and a fisher-trap closed on one of his hind feet. With a snarl he dropped Wapoos and turned upon it, SNAP—SNAP—SNAP went three more of Jacques's nest of traps. Two of them missed. The third caught him by a front paw. As he had caught Wapoos, and as he had killed the fisher-cat, so now he seized this new and savage enemy between his jaws. His fangs crunched on the cold steel; he literally tore it from his paw so that blood streamed forth and strained the snow red. Madly he twisted himself to get at his hind foot. On this foot the fisher-trap had secured a hold that was unbreakable. He ground it between his jaws until the blood ran from his mouth. He was fighting it when Le Beau came out from behind a clump of spruce twenty yards away with The Killer at his heels.

The Brute stopped. He was panting, and his eyes were aflame. Two hundred yards away he had heard the clinking of the trap-chain.

"Ow! he is there," he gasped, tightening his hold on The Killer's lead thong. "He is there, Netah, you Red Eye! That is the robber devil you are to kill—almost. I will unfasten you, and then—Go To!"

Miki, no longer fighting the trap, was eyeing them as they advanced. In this moment of peril he felt no fear of the man. In his veins the hot blood raged with a killing madness. The truth leapt upon him in a flash of instinctive awakening. These two were his enemies instead of the thing on his foot—the man-beast, and Netah, The Killer. He remembered—as if it were yesterday. This was not the first time he had seen a man with a club in his hand. And Le Beau held a club. But he was not afraid. His steady eyes watched Netah. Unleashed by his master, The Killer stood on stiff legs a dozen feet away, the wiry crest along his spine erect, his muscles tense.

Miki heard the man-beast's voice.

"Go to, you devil! Go To!"

Miki waited, without the quiver of a muscle. Thus much he had learned of his hard lessons in the wilderness—to wait, and watch, and use his cunning. He was flat on his belly, his nose between his forepaws. His lips were drawn back a little, just a little; but he made no sound, and his eyes were as steady as two points of flame. Le Beau stared. He felt suddenly a new thrill, and it was not the thrill of his desire for vengeance. Never had he seen a lynx or a fox or a wolf in a trap like that. Never had he seen a dog with eyes like the eyes that were on Netah. For a moment he held his breath.

Foot by foot, and then almost inch by inch, The Killer crept in. Ten feet, eight, six—and all that time Miki made no move, never winked an eye. With a snarl like that of a tiger, Netah came at him.

What happened then was the most marvellous thing that Jacques Le Beau had ever seen. So swiftly that his eyes could scarcely follow the movement, Miki had passed like a flash under the belly of Netah, and turning then at the end of his trap chain he was at The Killer's throat before Le Beau could have counted ten. They were down, and The Brute gripped the club in his hand and stared like one fascinated. He heard the grinding crunch of jaws, and he knew they were the Wild Dog's jaws; he heard a snarl choking slowly into a wheezing sob of agony, and he knew that the sound came from The Eller. The blood rose into his face. The red fire in his eyes grew livid—a blaze of exultation, of triumph.

"TONNERRE DE DIEU! he is choking the life out of Netah!" he gasped. "NON, I have never seen a dog like that. I will keep him alive; and he shall fight Durant's Poos over at Post Fort O' God! By the belly of Saint Gris, I say—"

The Killer was as good as dead if left another minute. With upraised club Le Beau advanced. As he sank his fangs deeper into Netah's throat Miki saw the new danger out of the corner of his eye. He loosed his jaws and swung himself free of The Killer as the club descended. He only partly evaded the smashing blow, which caught him on the shoulder and knocked him down. Quick as a flash he was on his feet and had lunged at Le Beau. The Frenchman was a master with the club. All his life he had used it, and he brought it around in a sudden side-swing that landed with terrific force against Miki's head. The blood spurted from his mouth and nostrils. He was dazed and half blinded. He leapt again, and the club caught him once more. He heard Le Beau's ferocious cry of joy. A third, a fourth, and a fifth time he went down under the club, and Le Beau no longer laughed, but swung his weapon with a look that was half fear in his eyes. The sixth time the club missed, and Miki's jaws closed against The Brute's chest, ripping away the thick coat and shirt as if they had been of paper, and leaving on Le Beau's skin a bleeding gash. Ten inches more—a little better vision in his blood-dimmed eyes—and he would have reached the man's throat. A great cry rose out of Le Beau. For an instant he felt the appalling nearness of death.

"Netah! Netah!" he cried, and swung the club wildly.

Netah did not respond. It may be that in this moment he sensed the fact that it was his master who had made him into a monster. About him was the wilderness, opening its doors of freedom. When Le Beau called again The Killer was slinking away, dripping blood as he went—and this was the last that Le Beau saw of him. Probably he joined the wolves, for The Killer was a quarter-strain wild.

Le Beau got no more than a glimpse of him as he disappeared. His club-arm shot out again, a clean miss; and this time it was pure chance that saved him. The trap-chain caught, and Miki fell back when his hot breath was almost at The Brute's jugular. He fell upon his side. Before he could recover himself the club was pounding his head into the snow. The world grew black. He no longer had the power to move. Lying as if dead he still heard over him the panting, exultant voice of the man-beast. For Le Beau, black though his heart was, could not keep back a prayerful cry of thankfulness that he was victor—and had missed death, though by a space no wider than the link of a chain.

XVII

Nanette, the woman, saw Jacques come out of the edge of the timber late in the afternoon, dragging something on the snow behind him. In her heart, ever since her husband had begun to talk about him, she had kept secret to herself a pity for the wild dog. Long before the last baby had come she had loved a dog. It was this dog that had given her the only real affection she had known in the company of The Brute, and with barbarous cruelty Le Beau had driven it from her. Nanette herself had encouraged it to seek freedom in the wilderness, as Netah had at last sought his. Therefore she had prayed that the wild dog of the trapline might escape.

As Le Beau came nearer she saw that what he drew after him upon the snow was a sledge-drag made of four lengths of sapling, and when, a moment later, she looked down at its burden, she gave a little cry of horror.

Miki's four feet were tied so firmly to the pieces of sapling that he could not move. A cord about his neck was fastened to one of the crossbars, and over his jaws Le Beau had improvised a muzzle of unbreakable BABICHE thong. He had done all this before Miki regained consciousness after the clubbing. The woman stared, and there was a sudden catch in her breath after the little cry that had fallen from her lips. Many times she had seen Jacques club his dogs, but never had she seen one clubbed like this. Miki's head and shoulders were a mass of frozen blood. And then she saw his eyes. They were looking straight up at her. She turned, fearing that Jacques might see what was in her face.

Le Beau dragged his burden straight into the cabin, and then stood back and rubbed his hands as he looked at Miki on the floor. Nanette saw that he was in a strangely good humour, and waited.

"By the Blessed Saints, but you should have seen him kill Netah—almost," he exulted. "Oui; he had him down by the throat quicker than you could flash your eye, and twice he was within an inch of my life when I fought him with the club. Dieu! I say, what will happen to Durant's dog when they meet at Post Fort O' God? I will make a side wager that he kills him before the second-hand of Le Facteur's watch, goes round twice. He is splendid! Watch him, Nanette, while I go make a corral for him alone. If I put him in with the pack he will kill them all."

Miki's eyes followed him as he disappeared through the cabin door. Then he looked swiftly back to Nanette. She had drawn nearer. Her eyes were shining as she bent over him. A snarl rose in Miki's throat, and died there. For the first time he was looking upon WOMAN. He sensed, all at once, a difference as vast as the world itself. In his bruised and broken body his heart stood still. Nanette spoke to him. Never in his life had he heard a voice like hers—soft and gentle, with a breaking sob in it; and then—miracle of miracles—she had dropped on her knees and her hands were at his head!

In that instant his spirit leapt back through the generations—back beyond his father, and his father's father; back to that far day when the blood in the veins of his race was "just dog," and he romped with children, and listened to the call of woman, and worshipped at the shrine of humankind. And now the woman had run quickly to the stove, and was back again with a dish of warm water and a soft cloth, and was bathing his head, talking to him all the time in that gentle, half-sobbing voice of pity and of love. He closed his eyes—no longer afraid. A great sigh heaved out of his body. He wanted to put out his tongue and lick the slim white hands that were bringing him peace and comfort. And then the strangest thing of all happened. In the crib the baby sat up and began to prattle. It was a new note to Miki, a new song of Life's spring-tide to him, but it thrilled him as nothing else in all the world had ever thrilled him before. He opened his eyes wide—and whined.

A laugh of joy—new and strange even to herself—came into the woman's voice, and she ran to the crib and returned with the baby in her arms. She knelt down beside him again, and the baby, at sight of this strange plaything on the floor, thrust out its little arms, and kicked its tiny moccasined feet, and cooed and laughed and squirmed until Miki strained at his thongs to get a little nearer that he might touch this wonderful creature with his nose. He forgot his pain. He no longer sensed the agony of his bruised and beaten jaws. He did not feel the numbness of his tightly bound and frozen legs. Every instinct in him was centred in these two.

And the woman, now, was beautiful. She UNDERSTOOD; and the gentle heart throbbed in her bosom, forgetful of The Brute. Her eyes glowed with the soft radiance of stars. Into her pale cheeks came a sweet flush. She sat the baby down, and with the cloth and warm water continued to bathe Miki's head. Le Beau, had he been human, must have worshipped her then as she knelt there, all that was pure and beautiful in motherhood, an angel of mercy, radiant for a moment in her forgetfulness of HIM. And Le Beau DID enter—and see her—so quietly that for a space she did not realize his presence; and with him staring down on her she continued to talk and laugh and half sob, and the baby kicked and prattled and flung out its little arms wildly in the joy of these exciting moments.

Le Beau's thick lips drew back in an ugly leer, and he gave a savage curse. Nanette flinched as if struck a blow.

"Get up, you fool!" he snarled.

She obeyed, shrinking back with the baby in her arms. Miki saw the change, and the greenish fire returned into his eyes when he caught sight of Le Beau. A deep and wolfish snarl rose in his throat.

Le Beau turned on Nanette. The glow and the flush had not quite gone from her eyes and cheeks as she stood with the baby hugged up to her breast, and her big shining braid had fallen over her shoulder, glistening with a velvety fire in the light that came through the western window. But Le Beau saw nothing of this.

"If you make a Poos (a house-kitten) of that dog—a thing like you made of Minoo, the breed-bitch, I will—"

He did not finish, but his huge hands were clinched, and there was an ugly passion in his eyes. Nanette needed no more than that. She understood. She had received many blows, but there was the memory of one that never left her, night or day. Some day, if she could ever get to Post Fort O' God, and had the courage, she would tell LE FACTEUR of that blow—how Jacques Le Beau, her husband, struck it at the nursing time, and her bosom was so hurt that the baby of two years ago had died. She would tell it, when she knew she and the baby would be safe from the vengeance of the Brute. And only LE FACTEUR—the Big Man at Post Fort O' God a hundred miles away—was powerful enough to save her.

It was well that Le Beau did not read this thought in her mind now. With his warning he turned to Miki and dragged him out of the cabin to a cage made of saplings in which the winter before he had kept two live foxes. A small chain ten feet in length he fastened around Miki's neck and then to one of the sapling bars before he thrust his prisoner inside the door of the prison and freed him by cutting the BABICHE thongs with a knife.

For several minutes after that Miki lay still while the blood made its way slowly through his numbed and half-frozen limbs. At last he staggered to his feet, and then it was that Le Beau chuckled jubilantly and turned back to the cabin.

And now followed many days that were days of hell and torment for him—an unequal struggle between the power of The Brute and the spirit of the Dog.

"I must break you—Ow! by the Christ! I WILL break you!"—Le Beau would say time and again when he came with the club and the whip. "I will make you crawl to me—OUI, and when I say fight you will fight!"

It was a small cage, so small that Miki could not get away from the reach of the club and the whip. They maddened him—for a time, and Le Beau's ugly soul was filled with joy as Miki launched himself again and again at the sapling bars, tearing at them with his teeth and frothing blood like a wolf gone mad. For twenty years Le Beau had trained fighting dogs, and this was his way. So he had done with Netah until The Killer was mastered, and at his call crept to him on his belly.

Three times, from a window in the cabin, Nanette looked forth on these horrible struggles between the man and the dog, and the third time she buried her face in her arms and sobbed; and when Le Beau came in and found her crying he dragged her to the window and made her look out again at Miki, who lay bleeding and half dead in the cage. It was a morning on which he started the round of his traps, and he was always gone until late the following day. And never was he more than well out of sight than Nanette would run out and go to the cage.

It was then that Miki forgot The Brute. At times so beaten and blinded that he could scarcely stand or see, he would crawl to the bars of the cage and caress the soft hands that Nanette held in fearlessly to him. And then, after a little, Nanette began to bring the baby out with her, bundled up like a little Eskimo, and in his joy Miki whimpered and wagged his tail and grovelled in his worship before these two.

It was in the second week of his captivity that the wonderful thing happened. Le Beau was gone, and there was a raging blizzard outside to which Nanette dared not expose the baby. So she went to the cage, and with a heart that beat wildly, she unbarred the door—and brought Miki into the cabin! If Le Beau should ever discover what she had done—!

The thought made her shiver.

After this first time she brought him into the cabin again and again. Once her heart stood still when Le Beau saw blood on the floor, and his eyes shot at her suspiciously. Then she lied.

"I cut my finger she said," and a moment later, with her back to him, she DID cut it, and when Jacques looked at her hand he saw a cloth about the finger, with blood-stain on it.

After that Nanette always watched the floor carefully.

More and more this cabin, with the woman and the baby in it, became a paradise for Miki. Then came the time when Nanette dared to keep him in the cabin with her all night, and lying close to the precious cradle Miki never once took his eyes from her. It was late when she prepared for bed. She changed into a long, soft robe, and then, sitting near Miki, with her bare little feet in the fireglow, she took down her wonderful hair and began brushing it. It was the first time Miki had seen this new and marvellous garment about her. It fell over her shoulders and breast and almost to the floor in a shimmering glory, and the scent of it was so sweet that Miki crept a few inches nearer, and whimpered softly. After she had done brushing it Miki watched her as her slim fingers plaited it into two braids; and then, before she put the light out, a still more curious thing happened. She went to her bed, made of saplings, against the wall, and from its hiding place under the blankets drew forth tenderly a little ivory Crucifix. With this in her hands she knelt upon the log floor, and Miki listened to her prayer. He did not know, but she was asking God to be good to her baby—the little Nanette in the crib.

After that she cuddled the baby up in her arms, and put out the light, and went to bed; and through all the hours of the night Miki made no sound that would waken them.

In the morning, when Nanette opened her eyes, she found Miki with his head resting on the edge of the bed, close to the baby that was nestled against her bosom.

That morning, as she built the fire, something strange and stirring in Nanette's breast made her sing. Le Beau would be away until dark that night, and she would never dare to tell him what she and the baby and the dog were going to do. It was her birthday. Twenty-six; and it seemed to her that she had lived the time of two lives! And eight of those years with The Brute! But to-day they would celebrate, they three. All the morning the cabin was filled with a new spirit—a new happiness.

Years ago, before she had met Le Beau, the Indians away back on the Waterfound had called Nanette "Tanta Penashe" ("the Little Bird") because of the marvellous sweetness of her voice. And this morning

JAMES OLIVER CURWOOD

she sang as she prepared the birthday feast; the sun flooded through the windows, and Miki whimpered happily and thumped his tail, and the baby cackled and crowed, and The Brute was forgotten. In that forgetfulness Nanette was a girl again, sweet and beautiful as in those days when old Jackpine, the Cree—who was now dead—had told her that she was born of the flowers. The wonderful dinner was ready at last, and to the baby's delight Nanette induced Miki to sit on a chair at the table. He felt foolish there, and he looked so foolish that Nanette laughed until her long dark lashes were damp with tears; and then, when Miki slunk down from the chair, feeling his shame horribly, she ran to him and put her arms around him and pleaded with him until he took his place at the table again.

So the day passed until mid-afternoon, when Nanette cleared away all signs of the celebration and locked Miki in his cage. It was fortunate she was ahead of time, for scarcely was she done when Le Beau came into the edge of the clearing, and with him was Durant, his acquaintance and rival from the edge of the Barrens farther north. Durant had sent his outfit on to Port O' God by an Indian, and had struck south and west with two dogs and a sledge to visit a cousin for a day or two. He was on his way to the Post when he came upon Le Beau on his trapline.

Thus much Le Beau told Nanette, and Nanette looked at Durant with startled eyes. They were a good pair, Jacques and his guest, only that Durant was older. She had become somewhat accustomed to the brutality in Le Beau's face, but she thought that Durant was a monster. He made her afraid, and she was glad when they went from the cabin.

"Now I will show you the Bete that is going to kill your Poos as easily as your lead-whelp killed that rabbit to-day, m'sieu," exulted Jacques. "I have told you but you have not seen!"

And he took with him the club and the whip.

Like a tiger fresh out of the jungles Miki responded to the club and the whip to-day, until Durant himself stood aghast, and exclaimed under his breath: "Mon Dieu! he is a devil!"

From the window Nanette saw what was happening, and out of her rose a cry of anguish. Sudden as a burst of fire there arose in her— triumphant at last and unafraid—that thing which for years The Brute had crushed back: her womanhood resurrected! Her soul broken free of its shackles! Her faith, her strength, her courage! She turned from the window and ran to the door, and out over the snow to the cage; and for the first time in her life she struck at Le Beau, and beat fiercely at the arm that was wielding the club.

"You beast!" she cried. "I tell you, you SHALL NOT! Do you hear? You SHALL NOT!"

Paralyzed with amazement, The Brute stood still. Was this Nanette, his slave? This wonderful creature with eyes that were glowing fire and defiance, and a look in her face that he had never seen in any woman's face before? NON—impossible! Hot rage rose in him, and with a single sweep of his powerful arm he flung her back so that she fell to the earth. With a wild curse he lifted the bar of the cage door.

"I will kill him, now; I will KILL him!" he almost shrieked. "And it is YOU—YOU—you she-devil! who shall eat his heart alive! I will force it down your throat: I will—"

He was dragging Miki forth by the chain. The club rose as Miki's head came through. In another instant it would have beaten his head to a pulp—but Nanette was between it and the dog like a flash, and the blow went wild. It was with his fist that Le Beau struck out now, and the blow caught Nanette on the shoulder and sent her frail body down with a crash. The Brute sprang upon her. His fingers gripped in her thick, soft hair.

And then—

From Durant came a warning cry. It was too late. A lean gray streak of vengeance and retribution, Miki was at the end of his chain and at Le Beau's throat. Nanette HEARD! Through dazed eyes she SAW! She reached out gropingly and struggled to her feet, and looked just once down upon the snow. Then, with a terrible cry, she staggered toward the cabin.

When Durant gathered courage to drag Le Beau out of Miki's reach Miki made no movement to harm him. Again, perhaps, it was the Beneficent Spirit that told him his duty was done. He went back into his cage, and lying there on his belly looked forth at Durant.

And Durant, looking at the blood-stained snow and the dead body of The Brute, whispered to himself again:

"MON DIEU! he is a devil!"

In the cabin, Nanette was upon her knees before the crucifix.

XVIII

There are times when death is a shock, but not a grief. And so it was with Nanette Le Beau. With her own eyes she had looked upon the terrible fate of her husband, and it was not in her gentle soul to weep or wish him alive again. At last there had overtaken him what Le Bon Dieu had intended him to receive some day: justice. And for the baby's sake more than her own Nanette was not sorry. Durant, whose soul was only a little less wicked than the dead man's, had not even waited for a prayer—had not asked her what to do. He had chopped a hole in the frozen earth and had buried Le Beau almost before his body was cold. And Nanette was not sorry for that. The Brute was gone. He was gone for ever. He would never strike her again. And because of the baby she offered up a prayer of gratitude to God.

In his prison-cage of sapling bars Miki cringed on his belly at the end of his chain. He had scarcely moved since those terrible moments in which he had torn the life out of the man-brute's throat. He had not even growled at Durant when he dragged the body away. Upon him had fallen a fearful and overwhelming oppression. He was not thinking of his own brutal beatings, or of the death which Le Beau had been about to inflict upon him with the club; he did not feel the presence of pain in his bruised and battered body, nor in his bleeding jaws and whip-lashed eyes. He was thinking of Nanette, the woman. Why had she run away with that terrible cry when he killed the man-beast? Was it not the man-beast who had struck her down, and whose hands were at her white throat when he sprang the length of his chain and tore out his jugular? Then why was it that she ran away, and did not come back?

He whimpered softly.

The afternoon was almost gone, and the early gloom of mid-winter night in the Northland was settling thickly over the forests. In that gloom the dark face of Durant appeared at the bars of Miki's prison. Instinctively Miki had hated this foxhunter from the edge of the Barrens, just as he had hated Le Beau, for in their brutish faces as well as in their hearts they were like brothers. Yet he did not growl at Durant as he peered through. He did not even move.

"Ugh! Le Diable!" shuddered Durant.

Then he laughed. It was a low, terrible laugh, half smothered in his coarse black beard, and it sent an odd chill through Miki.

He turned after that and went into the cabin.

Nanette rose to meet him, her great dark eyes glowing in a face dead white. She had not yet risen above the shock of Le Beau's tragic death, and yet in those eyes there was already something re-born. It had not been there when Durant came to the cabin with Le Beau that afternoon. He looked at her strangely as she stood with the baby in her arms. She was another Nanette. He felt uneasy. Why was it that a few hours ago he had laughed boldly when her husband had cursed her and said vile things in her presence—and now he could not meet the steady gaze of her eyes? DIEU! he had never before observed how lovely she was! He drew himself together, and stated the business in his mind.

"You will not want the dog," he said. "I will take him away."

Nanette did not answer. She seemed scarcely to be breathing as she looked at him. It seemed to him that she was waiting for him to explain; and then the inspiration to lie leapt into his mind.

"You know, there was to be the big fight between HIS dog and mine at Post Fort O' God at the New Year carnival," he went on, shuffling his heavy feet. "For that, Jacques—your husband—was training the wild dog. And when I saw that OOCHUN—that wolf devil—tearing at the bars of the cage I knew he would kill my dog as a fox kills a rabbit. So we struck a bargain, and for the two cross foxes and the ten red which I have outside I bought him." (The VRAISEMBLANCE of his lie gave him courage. It sounded like truth, and Jacques, the dead man, was not there to repudiate his claim.) "So he is mine," he finished a little exultantly, "and I will take him to the Post, and will fight him against any dog or wolf in all the North. Shall I bring in the skins, MADAME?"

"He is not for sale," said Nanette, the glow in her eyes deepening. "He is my dog—mine and the baby's. Do you understand, Henri Durant? HE IS NOT FOR SALE!"

"OUI," gasped Durant, amazed.

"And when you reach Post Fort O' God, m'sieu, you will tell LE FACTEUR that Jacques is dead, and how he died, and say that some one must be sent for the baby and me. We will stay here until then."

"OUI," said Durant again, backing to the door.

He had never seen her like that. He wondered how Jacques Le Beau could swear at her, and strike her. For himself, he was afraid. Standing there with those wonderful eyes and white face, with the baby in her arms, and her shining hair over her breasts, she made him think of a picture he had once seen of the Blessed Lady.

He went out through the door and back to the sapling cage where Miki lay. Softly he spoke through the bars.

"Ow, Bete" he called; "she will not sell you. She keeps you because you fought for her, and killed Mon Ami, Jacques Le Beau. And so I must take you my own way. In a little while the moon will be up, and then I will slip a noose over your head at the end of a pole, and will choke you so quickly she will not hear a sound. And who will know where you are gone, if the cage door is left open? And you will fight for me at Post Fort O' God. Mon Dieu! how you will fight! I swear it will do the ghost of Jacques Le Beau good to see what happens there."

He went away, to where he had left his light sledge and two dogs in the edge of the timber, and waited for the moon to rise.

Still Miki did not move, A light had appeared in the window of the cabin, and his eyes were fixed on it yearningly as the low whine gathered in his throat again. His world no longer lay beyond that window. The Woman and the baby had obliterated in him all desire but to be with them.

In the cabin Nanette was thinking of him—and of Durant. The man's words came to her again, vividly, significantly: "You Will Not Want The Dog." Yes, all the forest people would say that same thing—even Le Facteur himself, when he heard. She Would Not Want The Dog! And why not? Because he had killed Jacques Le Beau, her husband, in defence of her? Because he had freed her from the bondage of The Brute? Because God had sent him to the end of his chain in that terrible moment that the baby Nanette might live, as the Other had not, and that she might grow up with laughter on her lips instead of sobs? In her there rose suddenly a thought that fanned the new flame in her heart. It Must have been Le Bon Dieu! Others might doubt, but she—never. She recalled all that Le Beau had told her about the wild dog—how for many days he had robbed the traps, and the terrific fight he had made when at last he was caught. And of all that The Brute had said there stood out most the words he had spoken one day.

"He is a devil, but he was not born of wolf. Non, some time, a long time ago, he was a white man's dog."

A White Man's Dog!

Her soul thrilled. Once—a long time ago—he had known a master with a white heart, just as she had known a girlhood in which the flowers bloomed and the birds sang. She tried to look back, but she could not see very far. She could not vision that day, less than a year ago, when Miki, an angular pup, came down out of the Farther North with Challoner; she could not vision the strange comradeship between the pup and Neewa, the little black bear cub, nor that tragic day when they had fallen out of Challoner's canoe into the swift stream that had carried them over the waterfall and into the Great Adventure which had turned Neewa into a grown bear and Miki into a wild dog. But in her heart she FELT the things which she could not see. Miki had not come by chance. Something greater than that had sent him.

She rose quietly, so that she would not waken the baby in the crib, and opened the door. The moon was just rising over the forest and through the glow of it she went to the cage. She heard the dog's joyous whine, and then she felt the warm caress of his tongue upon her bare hands as she thrust them between the sapling bars.

"NON, NON; you are not a devil," she cried softly, her voice filled with a strange tremble. "O-o-ee, my SOKETAAO, I prayed, PRAYED—and you came. Yes, on my knees each night I prayed to Our Blessed Lady that she might have mercy on my baby, and make the sun in heaven shine for her through all time. AND YOU CAME! And the dear God does not send devils in answer to prayer. NON; never!"

And Miki, as though some spirit had given him the power to understand, rested the weight of his bruised and beaten head on her hands.

From the edge of the forest Durant was watching. He had caught the flash of light from the door and had seen Nanette go to the cage, and his eyes did not leave her until she returned into the cabin. He laughed as he went to his fire and finished making the WAHGUN he was fastening to the end of a long pole. This WAHGUN and the pole added to his own cleverness were saving him twelve good fox skins, and he continued to chuckle there in the fireglow as he thought how easy it was to beat a woman's wits. Nanette was a fool to refuse the pelts, and Jacques was—dead. It was a most lucky combination of circumstances for him. Fortune had surely come his way. On LE BETE, as he called the wild dog, he would gamble all that he possessed in the big fight. And he would win.

He waited until the light in the cabin went out before he approached the cage again. Miki heard him coming. At a considerable distance he saw him, for the moon was already turning the night into day. Durant knew the ways of dogs. With them he employed a superior reason where Le Beau had used the club and the rawhide. So he came up openly and boldly, and, as if by accident, dropped the end of the pole between the bars. With his hands against the cage, apparently unafraid, he began talking in a casual way. He was different from Le Beau. Miki watched him closely for a space and then let his eyes rest again on the darkened cabin window. Stealthily Durant began to take advantage of his opportunity. A little at a time he moved the end of the pole until it was over Miki's head, with the deadly bowstring and its open noose hanging down. He was an adept in the use of the WAHGUN. Many foxes and wolves, and even a bear, he had caught that way. Miki, numbed by the cold, scarcely felt the BABICHE noose as it settled softly about his neck. He did not see Durant brace himself, with his feet against the running-log of the cage.

Then, suddenly, Durant lurched himself backward, and it seemed to Miki as though a giant trap of steel had closed about his neck. Instantly his wind was cut off. He could make no sound as he struggled frantically to free himself. Hand over hand Durant dragged him to the bars, and there, with his feet still braced, he choked with his whole weight until— when at last he let up on the WAHGUN—Miki collapsed as if dead. Ten seconds later Durant was looping a muzzle over his closed jaws. He left the cage door open when he went back to his sledge, carrying Miki in his arms. Nanette's slow wits would never guess, he told himself. She would think that LE BÊTE had escaped into the forest.

It was not his scheme to club Miki into serfdom, as Le Beau had failed to do. Durant was wiser than that. In his crude and merciless way he had come to know certain phenomena of the animal mind. He was not a psychologist; oh the other hand brutality had not utterly blinded him. So, instead of lashing Miki to the sledge as Le Beau had fastened him to his improvised drag, Durant made his captive comfortable, covering him with a warm blanket before he began his journey eastward. He made sure, however, that there was no flaw in the muzzle about Miki's jaws, and that the free end of the chain to which he was still fastened was well hitched to the Gee-bar of his sledge.

When these things were done Durant set off in the direction of Fort O' God, and if Jacques Le Beau could have seen him then he would have had good reason to guess at his elation. By taint of birth and blood Durant was a gambler first, and a trapper afterward. He set his traps that he might have the thrill of wagering his profits, and for half a dozen successive years he had won at the big annual dog fight at Post Fort O' God. But this year he had been half afraid. His fear had not been of Jacques Le Beau and Netah, but of the halfbreed away over on Red Belly Lake. Grouse Piet was the halfbreed's name, and the "dog" that he was going to put up at the fight was half wolf. Therefore, in the foolish eagerness of his desire, had Durant offered two cross foxes and ten reds—the price of five dogs and not one—for the possession of Le Beau's wild dog. And now that he had him for nothing, and Nanette was poorer by twelve skins, he was happy. For he had now a good match for Grouse Piet's half wolf, and he would chance his money and his credit at the Post to the limit.

When Miki came back to his senses Durant stopped his dogs, for he had been watching closely for this moment. He bent over the sledge and began talking, not in Le Beau's brutal way, but in a careless chummy sort of voice, and with his mittened hand he patted his captive's head. This was a new thing to Miki, for he knew that it was not the hand of Nanette, but of a man-beast, and the softness of his nest in the blanket, over which Henri had thrown a bear skin, was also new. A short time ago he was frozen and stiff. Now he was warm and comfortable. So he did not move. And Durant exulted in his cleverness. He did not travel far in the night, but stopped four or five miles from Nanette's cabin, and built a fire. Over this he boiled coffee and roasted meat. He allowed the meat to roast slowly, turning it round and round on a wooden spit, so that the aroma of it grew thick and inviting in the air. He had fastened his two sledge dogs fifty paces away, but the sledge was close to the fire, and he watched the effect on Miki of the roasting meat. Since the days of his puppyhood with Challoner a smell like that which came from the meat had not filled Miki's nostrils, and at last Durant saw him lick his chops and heard the click of his teeth. He chuckled in his beard. Still he waited another quarter of an hour. Then he pulled the meat off the spit, cut it up, and gave a half of it to Miki. And Miki ate it ravenously.

A clever man was Henri Durant!

XIX

During the last few days in December all trails for ten thousand square miles around led to Post Fort O' God. It was the eve of Ooske Pipoon—of the New Year—the mid-winter carnival time of the people of the wilderness, when from teepees and cabins far and near come the trappers and their families to sell their furs and celebrate for a few days with others of their kind. To this New Year gathering men, women, and children look forward through long and weary months. The trapper's wife has no neighbour. Her husband's "line" is a little kingdom inviolate, with no other human life within many miles of it; so for the women the Ooske Pipoon is a time of rejoicing; for the children it is the "big circus," and for the men a reward for the labour and hardship of catching their fur. During these few days old acquaintanceships are renewed and new ones are made. It is here that the "news" of the trackless wilderness is spread, the news of deaths, of marriages, and of births; of tragic happenings that bring horror and grief and tears, and of others that bring laughter and joy. For the first and last time in all the seven months' winter the people of the forests "come to town." Indian, halfbreed, "blood," and white man, join in the holiday without distinction of colour or creed.

This year there was to be a great caribou roast, a huge barbecue, at Fort O' God, and by the time Henri Durant came within half a dozen miles of the Post the trails from north and south and east and west were beaten hard by the tracks of dogs and men. That year a hundred sledges came in from the forests, and with them were three hundred men and women and children and half a thousand dogs.

Durant was a day later than he had planned to be, but he had made good use of his time. For Miki, while still muzzled, now followed at the end of the babiche that was tied to Henri's sledge. In the afternoon of the third day after leaving Nanette Le Beau's cabin Durant turned off the main-travelled trail until he came to the shack of Andre Ribon, who kept the Factor and his people at the Post supplied with fresh meat. Andre, who was becoming over-anxious at Durant's delay, was still waiting when his friend came. It was here that Henri's Indian had left his fighting dog, the big husky. And here he left Miki, locked in Andre's shack. Then the two men went on to the Post which was only a mile away.

Neither he nor Ribon returned that night. The cabin was empty. And with the beginning of dusk Miki began to hear weird and strange sounds which grew louder as darkness settled deeper. It was the sound of the carnival at the Post—the distant tumult of human voice mingled with the howling of a hundred dogs. He had never heard anything like it before, and for a long time he listened without moving. Then he stood up like a man before the window with this fore-paws resting against the heavy sash. Ribon's cabin was at the crest of a knoll that over-looked the frozen lake, and far off, over the tops of the scrub timber that fringed the edge of it, Miki saw the red glow in the sky made by a score of great camp fires. He whined, and dropped on his four feet again. It was a long wait between that and another day. But the cabin was more comfortable than Le Beau's prison-cage had been. All through the night his restless slumber was filled with visions of Nanette and the baby.

Durant and Ribon did not return until nearly noon the next day. They brought with them fresh meat, of which Miki ate ravenously, for he was hungry. In an unresponsive way he tolerated the advances of these two. A second night he was left alone in the cabin. When Durant and Ribon came back again in the early dawn they brought with them a cage four feet square made of small birch saplings. The open door of this cage they drew close to the door of the cabin, and by means of a chunk of fresh meat Miki was induced to enter through it. Instantly the trap fell, and he was a prisoner. The cage was already fastened on a wide toboggan, and scarcely was the sun up when Miki was on his way to Fort O' God.

This was the big day at the carnival—the day of the caribou-roast and the fight. For many minutes before they came in sight of Fort O' God Miki heard the growing sound. It amazed him, and he stood up on his feet in his cage, rigid and alert, utterly unconscious of the men who were pulling him. He was looking ahead of them, and Durant chuckled exultantly as they heard him growl, and his teeth click.

"Oui, he will fight! He would fight Now," he chuckled.

They were following the shore of a lake. Suddenly they came around the end of a point, and all of Fort O' God lay on the rising shelf of the shore ahead of them. The growl died in Miki's throat. His teeth shut with a last click. For an instant his heart seemed to grow dead and still. Until this moment his world had held only half a dozen human beings. Now, so suddenly that he had no flash of warning, he saw a hundred of them, two hundred, three hundred. At sight of Durant and the cage a swarm of them began running down to the shore. And everywhere there were wolves, so many of them that his senses grew dazed as he stared. His cage was the centre of a clamouring, gesticulating horde of men and boys as it was dragged up the slope. Women began joining the crowd, many of them with small children in their arms. Then his journey came to an end. He was close to another cage, and in that cage was a beast like himself. Beside this cage there stood a tall, swarthy, shaggy-headed halfbreed who looked like a pirate. The man was Grouse Piet, Durant's rival.

A contemptuous leer was on his thick-lipped face as he looked at Miki. He turned, and to the group of dark-faced Indians and breeds about him he said something that roused a guttural laugh.

Durant's face flamed red.

"Laugh, you heathen," he challenged, "but don't forget that Henri Durant is here to take your bets!" Then he shook the two cross and ten red foxes in the face of Grouse Piet.

"Cover them, Grouse Piet," he cried. "And I have ten times more where they came from!"

With his muzzle lifted, Miki was sniffing the air. It was filled with strange scents, heavy with the odours of men, of dogs, and of the five huge caribou roasting on their spits fifteen feet over the big fires that were built under them. For ten hours those caribou would roast, turning slowly on spits as thick as a man's leg. The fight was to come before the feast.

For an hour the clatter and tumult of voices hovered about the two cages. Men appraised the fighters and made their bets, and Grouse Piet and Henri Durant made their throats hoarse flinging banter and contempt at each other. At the end of the hour the crowd began to thin out. In the place of men and women half a hundred dark-visaged little children crowded about the cages. It was not until then that Miki caught glimpses of the hordes of beasts fastened in ones and twos and groups in the edge of the clearing. His nostrils had at last caught the distinction. They were not wolves. They were like himself.

It was a long time before his eyes rested steadily on the wolf-dog in the other cage. He went to the edge of his bars and sniffed. The wolf-dog thrust his gaunt muzzle toward him. He made Miki think of the huge wolf he had fought one day on the edge of the cliff, and instinctively he showed his fangs, and snarled. The wolf-dog snarled back. Henri Durant rubbed his hands exultantly, and Grouse Piet laughed softly.

"Oui; they will F‌ɪɢʜᴛ!" said Henri again.

"Ze wolf, he will fight, oui," said Grouse Piet. "But your dog, m'sieu, he be vair seek, lak a puppy, w'en ze fight come!"

A little later Miki saw a white man standing close to his cage. It was MacDonnell, the Scotch factor. He gazed at Miki and the wolf-dog with troubled eyes. Ten minutes later, in the little room which he had made his office, he was saying to a younger man:

"I'd like to stop it, but I can't. They wouldn't stand for it. It would lose us half a season's catch of fur. There's been a fight like this at Fort O' God for the last fifty years, and I don't suppose, after all, that it's any worse than one of the prize fights down there. Only, in this case—"

"They kill," said the younger man.

"Yes, that's it. Usually one of the dogs dies."

The younger man knocked the ash out of his pipe.

"I love dogs," he said, simply. "There'll never be a fight at my post, Mac—unless it's between men. And I'm not going to see this fight, because I'm afraid I'd kill some one if I did."

XX

It was two o'clock in the afternoon. The caribou were roasting brown. In two more hours the feast would begin. The hour of the fight was at hand.

In the centre of the clearing three hundred men, women, and children were gathered in a close circle about a sapling cage ten feet square. Close to this cage, one at each side, were drawn the two smaller cages. Beside one of these cages stood Henri Durant; beside the other, Grouse Piet. They were not bantering now. Their faces were hard and set. And three hundred pairs of eyes were staring at them, and three hundred pairs of ears waiting for the thrilling signal.

It came—from Grouse Piet.

With a swift movement Durant pulled up the door of Miki's cage. Then, suddenly, he prodded him from behind with a crotched stick, and with a single leap Miki was in the big cage. Almost at the same instant the wolf-dog leapt from Grouse Piet's cage, and the two faced each other in the arena.

With the next breath he drew Durant could have groaned. What happened in the following half minute was a matter of environment with Miki. In the forest the wolf-dog would have interested him to the exclusion of everything else, and he would have looked upon him as another Netah or a wild wolf. But in his present surroundings the idea of fighting was the last to possess him. He was fascinated by that grim and waiting circle of faces closing in the big cage; he scrutinized it, turning his head sharply from point to point, as if hoping to see Nanette and the baby, or even Challoner his first master. To the wolf-dog Grouse Piet had given the name of Taao, because of the extraordinary length of his fangs; and of Taao, to Durant's growing horror, Miki was utterly oblivious after that first head-on glance. He trotted to the edge of the cage and thrust his nose between the bars, and a taunting laugh rose out of Grouse Piet's throat. Then he began making a circle of the cage, his sharp eyes on the silent ring of faces. Taao stood in the centre of the cage, and not once did his reddish eyes leave Miki. What was outside of the cage held small interest for him. He understood his business, and murder was bred in his heart. For a space during which Durant's heart beat like a hammer Taao turned, as if on a pivot, following Miki's movement, and the crest on his spine stood up like bristles.

Then Miki stopped, and in that moment Durant saw the end of all his hopes. Without a sound the wolf-dog was at his opponent. A bellow rose from Grouse Piet's lips. A deep breath passed through the circle of spectators, and Durant felt a cold chill run up his back to the roots of his hair. What happened in the next instant made men's hearts stand still. In that first rush Miki should have died. Grouse Piet expected him to die, and Durant expected him to die. But in the last fractional bit of the second in which the wolf-dog's jaws closed, Miki was transformed into a thing of living lightning. No man had ever seen a movement swifter than that with which he turned on Taao. Their jaws clashed. There was a sickening grinding of bone, and in another moment they were rolling and twisting together on the earth floor. Neither Grouse Piet nor Durant could see what was happening. They forgot even their own bets in the horror of that fight. Never had there been such a fight at Fort O' God.

The sound of it reached to the Company's store. In the door, looking toward the big cage, stood the young white man. He heard the snarling, the clashing of teeth, and his jaws set heavily and a dull flame burned in his eyes. His breath came in a sudden gasp.

"DAMN!" he cried, softly.

His hands clenched, and he stepped slowly down from the door and went toward the cage. It was over when he made his way through the ring of spectators. The fight had ended as suddenly as it had begun, and Grouse Piet's wolf-dog lay in the centre of the cage with a severed jugular. Miki looked as though he might be dying. Durant had opened the door and had slipped a rope over his head, and outside the cage Miki stood swaying on his feet, red with blood, and half blind. His flesh was red and bleeding in a dozen places, and a stream of blood trickled from his mouth. A cry of horror rose to the young white man's lips as he looked down at him.

And then, almost in the same breath, there came a still stranger cry. "Good God! Miki—Miki—Miki—"

Beating upon his brain as if from a vast distance, coming to him through the blindness of his wounds, Miki heard that voice.

The VOICE! THE voice that had lived with him in all his dreams, the voice he had waited for, and searched for, and knew that some day he would find. The voice of Challoner, his master!

He dropped on his belly, whining, trying to see through the film of blood in his eyes; and lying there, wounded almost unto death, his tail thumped the ground in recognition. And then, to the amazement of all who beheld, Challoner was down upon his knees beside him, and his arms were about him, and Miki's lacerated tongue was reaching for his hands, his face, his clothes.

"Miki—Miki—Miki!"

Durant's hand fell heavily upon Challoner's shoulder.

It was like the touch of a red-hot iron to Challoner. In a flash he was on his feet, facing him.

"He's mine," Challoner cried, trying to hold back his passion. "He's mine you—you devil!"

And then, powerless to hold back his desire for vengeance, his clenched fist swung like a rock to Durant's heavy jaw, and the Frenchman went to the ground. For a moment Challoner stood over him, but he did not move. Fiercely he turned upon Grouse Piet and the crowd. Miki was cringing at his feet again. Pointing to him, Challoner cried loudly, so all could hear.

"He's my dog. Where this beast got him I don't know. But he's mine. Look for yourselves! See—see him lick my hand. Would he do that for Him? And look at that ear. There's no other ear in all the north cut like that. I lost him almost a year ago, but I'd know him among ten thousand by that ear. By God!—if I had known—"

He elbowed his way through the breeds and Indians, leading Miki by the rope Durant had slipped over the dog's head. He went to MacDonnell, and told him what had happened. He told of the preceding spring, and of the accident in which Miki and the bear cub were lost from his canoe and swept over the waterfall. After registering his claim against whatever Durant might have to say he went to the shack in which he was staying at Fort O' God.

An hour later Challoner sat with Miki's big head between his two hands, and talked to him. He had bathed and dressed his wounds, and Miki could see. His eyes were on his master's face, and his hard tail thumped the floor. Both were oblivious of the sounds of the revellers outside; the cries of men, the shouting of boys, the laughter of women, and the incessant barking of dogs. In Challoner's eyes there was a soft glow.

"Miki, old boy, you haven't forgotten a thing—not a dam' thing, have you? You were nothing but an onery-legged pup then, but you didn't forget! Remember what I told you, that I was going to take you and the cub down to the Girl? Do you remember? The Girl I said was an angel, and 'd love you to death, and all that? Well, I'm glad something happened—and you didn't go. It wasn't the same when I got back, an' SHE wasn't the same, Miki. Lord, she'd got married, AND HAD TWO KIDS! Think of that, old scout—Two! How the deuce could she have taken care of you and the cub, eh? And nothing else was the same, Boy. Three years in God's Country—up here where you burst your lungs just for the fun of drinking in air—changed me a lot, I guess. Inside a week I wanted to come back, Miki. Yessir, I was SICK to come back. So I came. And we're going to stick now, Miki. You're going with me up to that new Post the Company has given me. From now on we're pals. Understand, old scout, we're PALS!"

XXI

It was late the night of the big feast at Post Fort O' God that MacDonnell, the factor, sent for Challoner. Challoner was preparing for bed when an Indian boy pounded on the door of his shack and a moment later gave him the message. He looked at his watch. It was eleven o'clock. What could the Factor want of him at that hour, he wondered? Flat on his belly near the warm box stove Miki watched his new-found master speculatively as he pulled on his boots. His eyes were wide open now. Challoner had washed from him the blood of the terrific fight of that afternoon.

"Something to do with that devil of a Durant," growled Challoner, looking at the battle-scarred dog. "Well, if he hopes to get You again, Miki, he's barking up the wrong tree. You're MINE!"

Miki thumped his hard tail on the floor and wriggled toward his master in mute adoration. Together they went out into the night.

It was a night of white moonlight and a multitude of stars. The four great fires over which the caribou had roasted for the savage barbecue that day were still burning brightly. In the edge of the forest that ringed in the Post were the smouldering embers of a score of smaller fires. Back of these fires were faintly outlined the gray shadows of teepees and tents. In these shelters the three hundred halfbreeds and Indians who had come in from the forest trails to the New Year carnival at the Post were sleeping. Only here and there was there a movement of life. Even the dogs were quiet after the earlier hours of excitement and gluttony.

Past the big fires, with their huge spits still standing, Challoner passed toward the Factor's quarters. Miki sniffed at the freshly picked bones. Beyond these bones there was no sign of the two thousand pounds of flesh that had roasted that day on the spits. Men, women, children, and dogs had stuffed themselves until there was nothing left. It was the silence of Mutai—the "belly god"—the god who eats himself to sleep each night—that hovered strangely over this Post of Fort O' God, three hundred miles from civilization.

There was a light in the Factor's room, and Challoner entered with Miki at his heels. MacDonnell, the Scotchman, was puffing moodily on his pipe. There was a worried look in his ruddy face as the younger man seated himself, and his eyes were on Miki.

"Durant has been here," he said. "He's ugly. I'm afraid of trouble. If you hadn't struck him—"

Challoner shrugged his shoulders as he filled his own pipe from the Factor's tobacco.

"You see—you don't just understand the situation at Fort O' God," went on MacDonnell. "There's been a big dog fight here at New Year for the last fifty years. It's become a part of history, a part of Fort O' God itself, and that's why in my own fifteen years here I haven't tried to stop it. I believe it would bring on a sort of—revolution. I'd wager a half of my people would go to another post with their furs. That's why all the sympathy seems to be with Durant. Even Grouse Piet, his rival, tells him he's a fool to let you get away with him that way. Durant says that dog is His."

MacDonnell nodded at Miki, lying at Challoner's feet.

"Then he lies," said Challoner quietly.

"He says he bought him of Jacques Le Beau."

"Then Le Beau sold a dog that didn't belong to him."

For a moment MacDonnell was silent. Then he said:

"But that wasn't what I had you come over for, Challoner. Durant told me something that froze my blood to-night. Your outfit starts for your post up in the Reindeer Lake county to-morrow, doesn't it?"

"In the morning."

"Then could you, with one of my Indians and a team, arrange to swing around by way of the Jackson's Knee? You'd lose a week, but you could overtake your outfit before it reached the Reindeer—and it would be a mighty big favour to me. There's a—a HELL of a thing happened over there."

Again he looked at Miki.

"GAWD!" he breathed.

Challoner waited. He thought he saw a shudder pass through the Factor's shoulders.

"I'd go myself—I ought to, but this frosted lung of mine has made me sit tight this winter, Challoner. I OUGHT to go. Why—(a sudden glow shot into his eyes)—I knew this Nanette Le Beau when she was SO HIGH, fifteen years ago. I watched her grow up, Challoner. If I hadn't been married—then—I'd have fallen in love with her. Do you know her, Challoner? Did you ever see Nanette Le Beau?"

Challoner shook his head.

"An angel—if God ever made one," declared MacDonnell through his red beard. "She lived over beyond the Jackson's Knee with her father.

And he died, froze to death crossing Red Eye Lake one night. I've always thought Jacques Le Beau MADE her marry him after that. Or else she didn't know, or was crazed, or frightened at being alone. Anyway, she married him. It was five years ago I saw her last. Now and then I've heard things, but I didn't believe—not all of them. I didn't believe that Le Beau beat her, and knocked her down when he wanted to. I didn't believe he dragged her through the snow by her hair one day until she was nearly dead. They were just rumours, and he was seventy miles away. But I believe them now. Durant came from their place, and I guess he told me a whole lot of the truth—to save that dog."

Again he looked at Miki.

"You see, Durant tells me that Le Beau caught the dog in one of his traps, took him to his cabin, and tortured him into shape for the big fight. When Durant came he was so taken with the dog that he bought him, and it was while Le Beau was driving the dog mad in his cage to show his temper that Nanette interfered. Le Beau knocked her down, and then jumped on her and was pulling her hair and choking her when the dog went for him and killed him. That's the story. Durant told me the truth through fear that I'd have the dog shot if he was an out-and-out murderer. And that's why I want you to go by way of the Jackson's Knee. I want you to investigate, and I want you to do what you can for Nanette Le Beau. My Indian will bring her back to Port O' God."

With Scotch stoicism MacDonnell had repressed whatever excitement he may have felt. He spoke quietly. But the curious shudder went through his shoulders again. Challoner stared at him in blank amazement.

"You mean to say that Miki—this dog—has killed a man?"

"Yes. He killed him, Durant says, just as he killed Grouse Piet's wolf-dog in the big fight to-day. UGH!" As Challoner's eyes fell slowly upon Miki, the Factor added: "But Grouse Piet's dog was better than the man. If what I hear about Le Beau was true he's better dead than alive. Challoner, if you didn't think it too much trouble, and could go that way—and see Nanette—"

"I'll go," said Challoner, dropping a hand to Miki's head.

For half an hour after that MacDonnell told him the things he knew about Nanette Le Beau. When Challoner rose to go the Factor followed him to the door.

"Keep your eyes open for Durant," he warned. "That dog is worth more to him than all his winnings to-day, and they say his stakes were big. He won heavily from Grouse Piet, but the halfbreed is thick with him now. I know it. So watch out."

Out in the open space, in the light of the moon and stars, Challoner stood far a moment with Miki's forepaws resting against his breast. The dog's head was almost on a level with his shoulders.

"D'ye remember when you fell out of the canoe, Boy?" he asked softly. "Remember how you 'n' the cub were tied in the bow, an' you got to scrapping and fell overboard just above the rapids? Remember? By Jove! those rapids pretty near got ME, too. I thought you were dead, sure—both of you. I wonder what happened to the cub?"

Miki whined in response, and his whole body trembled.

"And since then you've killed a man," added Challoner, as if he still could not quite believe. "And I'm to take you back to the woman. That's the funny thing about it. You're going back to HER, and if she says kill you—"

He dropped Miki's forefeet and went on to the cabin. At the threshold a low growl rose in Miki's throat. Challoner laughed, and opened the door. They went in, and the dog's growl was a menacing snarl. Challoner had left his lamp burning low, and in the light of it he saw Henri Durant and Grouse Piet waiting for him. He turned up the wick, and nodded.

"Good evening. Pretty late for a call, isn't it?"

Grouse Piet's stolid face did not change its expression. It struck Challoner, as he glanced at him, that in head and shoulders he bore a grotesque resemblance to a walrus. Durant's eyes were dully ablaze. His face was swollen where Challoner had struck him. Miki, stiffened to the hardness of a knot, and still snarling under his breath, had crawled under Challoner's bunk. Durant pointed to him.

"We've come after that dog," he said.

"You can't have him, Durant," replied Challoner, trying hard to make himself appear at ease in a situation that sent a chill up his back. As he spoke he was making up his mind why Grouse Piet had come with Durant. They were giants, both of them: more than that—monsters. Instinctively he had faced them with the small table between them. "I'm sorry I lost my temper out there," he continued. "I shouldn't have struck you, Durant. It wasn't your fault—and I apologize. But the dog is mine. I lost him over in the Jackson's Knee country, and if Jacques Le Beau caught him in a trap, and sold him to you, he sold a dog that didn't belong to him. I'm willing to pay you back what you gave for him, just to be fair. How much was it?"

Grouse Piet had risen to his feet. Durant came to the opposite edge of the table, and leaned over it. Challoner wondered how a single blow had knocked him down.

"Non, he is not for sale." Durant's voice was low; so low that it seemed to choke him to get it out. It was filled with a repressed hatred. Challoner saw the great cords of his knotted hands bulging under the skin as he gripped the edge of the table. "M'sieu, we have come for that dog. Will you let us take him?"

"I will pay you back what you gave for him, Durant. I will add to the price."

"Non. He is mine. Will you give him back—Now?"

"No!"

Scarcely was the word out of his mouth when Durant flung his whole weight and strength against the table. Challoner had not expected the move—just yet. With a bellow of rage and hatred Durant was upon him, and under the weight of the giant he crashed to the floor. With them went the table and lamp. There was a vivid splutter of flame and the cabin was in darkness, except where the moon-light flooded through the one window. Challoner had looked for something different. He had expected Durant to threaten before he acted, and, sizing up the two of them, he had decided to reach the edge of his bunk during the discussion. Under the pillow was his revolver. It was too late now. Durant was on him, fumbling in the darkness for his throat, and as he flung one arm upward to get a hook around the Frenchman's neck he heard Grouse Piet throw the table back. The next instant they were rolling in the moonlight on the floor, and Challoner caught a glimpse of Grouse Piet's huge bulk bending over them. Durant's head was twisted under his arm, but one of the giant's hands had reached his throat. The halfbreed saw this, and he cried out something in a guttural voice. With a tremendous effort Challoner rolled himself and his adversary out of the patch of light into darkness again. Durant's thick neck cracked. Again Grouse Piet called out in that guttural, questioning voice. Challoner put every ounce of his energy into the crook of his arm, and Durant did not answer.

Then the weight of Grouse Piet fell upon them, and his great hands groped for Challoner's neck. His thick fingers found Durant's beard first, then fumbled for Challoner, and got their hold. Ten seconds of their terrific grip would have broken his neck. But the fingers never closed. A savage cry of agony burst from Grouse Piet's lips, and with that cry, ending almost in a scream, came the snap of great jaws and the rending snarl of fangs in the darkness. Durant heard, and with a great heave of his massive body he broke free from Challoner's grip, and leapt to his feet. In a flash Challoner was at his bunk, facing his enemies with the revolver in his hand.

Everything had happened quickly. Scarcely more than a minute had passed since the overturning of the table, and now, in the moment when the situation had turned in his favour, a sudden swift and sickening horror seized upon Challoner. Bloody and terrible there rose before him the one scene he had witnessed that day in the big cage where Miki and the wolf-dog had fought. And there—in that darkness of the cabin—

He heard a moaning cry and the crash of a body to the floor.

"Miki, Miki," he cried. "Here! Here!"

He dropped his revolver and sprang to the door, flinging it wide open.

"For God's sake get out!" he cried. "GET OUT!"

A bulk dashed past him into the night. He knew it was Durant. Then he leapt to the dark shadows on the floor and dug his two hands into the loose hide at the back of Miki's neck, dragging him back, and shouting his name. He saw Grouse Piet crawling toward the door. He saw him rise to his feet, silhouetted for a moment against the starlight, and stagger out into the night. And then he felt Miki's weight slinking down to the floor, and under his hands the dog's muscles grew limp and saggy. For two or three minutes he continued to kneel beside him before he closed the cabin door and lighted another lamp. He set up the overturned table and placed the lamp on it. Miki had not moved. He lay flat on his belly, his head between his forepaws, looking up at Challoner with a mute appeal in his eyes.

Challoner reached out his two arms.

"Miki!"

In an instant Miki was up against him, his forefeet against his breast, and with his arms about the dog's shoulders Challoner's eyes took in the floor. On it were wet splashes and bits of torn clothing.

His arms closed more tightly.

"Miki, old boy, I'm much obliged," he said.

XXII

The next morning Challoner's outfit of three teams and four men left north and west for the Reindeer Lake country on the journey to his new post at the mouth of the Cochrane. An hour later Challoner struck due west with a light sledge and a five-dog team for the Jackson's Knee. Behind him followed one of MacDonnell's Indians with the team that was to bring Nanette to Fort O' God.

He saw nothing more of Durant and Grouse Piet, and accepted MacDonnell's explanation that they had undoubtedly left the Post shortly after their assault upon him in the cabin. No doubt their disappearance had been hastened by the fact that a patrol of the Royal Northwest Mounted Police on its way to York Factory was expected at Fort O' God that day.

Not until the final moment of departure was Miki brought from the cabin and tied to the gee-bar of Challoner's sledge. When he saw the five dogs squatted on their haunches he grew rigid and the old snarl rose in his throat. Under Challoner's quieting words he quickly came to understand that these beasts were not enemies, and from a rather suspicious toleration of them he very soon began to take a new sort of interest in them. It was a friendly team, bred in the south and without the wolf strain.

Events had come to pass so swiftly and so vividly in Miki's life during the past twenty-four hours that for many miles after they left Fort O' God his senses were in an unsettled state of anticipation. His brain was filled with a jumble of strange and thrilling pictures. Very far away, and almost indistinct, were the pictures of things that had happened before he was made a prisoner by Jacques Le Beau. Even the memory of Neewa was fading under the thrill of events at Nanette's cabin and at Fort O' God. The pictures that blazed their way across his brain now were of men, and dogs, and many other things that he had never seen before. His world had suddenly transformed itself into a host of Henri Durants and Grouse Piets and Jacques Le Beaus, two-legged beasts who had clubbed him, and half killed him, and who had made him fight to keep the life in his body. He had tasted their blood in his vengeance. And he watched for them now. The pictures told him they were everywhere. He could imagine them as countless as the wolves, and as he had seen them crowded round the big cage in which he had slain the wolf-dog.

In all of this excited and distorted world there was only one Challoner, and one Nanette, and one baby. All else was a chaos of uncertainty and of dark menace. Twice when the Indian came up close behind them Miki whirled about with a savage snarl. Challoner watched him, and understood.

Of the pictures in his brain one stood out above all others, definite and unclouded, and that was the picture of Nanette. Yes, even above Challoner himself. There lived in him the consciousness of her gentle hands; her sweet, soft voice; the perfume of her hair and clothes and body—the WOMAN of her; and a part of the woman—as the hand is a part of the body—was the baby. It was this part of Miki that Challoner could not understand, and which puzzled him when they made camp that night. He sat for a long time beside the fire trying to bring back the old comradeship of the days of Miki's puppyhood. But he only partly succeeded. Miki was restive. Every nerve in his body seemed on edge. Again and again he faced the west, and always when he sniffed the air in that direction there came a low whine in his throat.

That night, with doubt in his heart, Challoner fastened him near the tent with a tough rope of babiche.

For a long time after Challoner had gone to bed Miki sat on his haunches close to the spruce to which he was fastened. It must have been ten o'clock, and the night was so still that the snap of a dying ember in the fire was like the crack of a whip to his ears. Miki's eyes were wide open and alert. Near the slowly burning logs, wrapped in his thick blankets, he could make out the motionless form of the Indian, asleep. Back of him the sledge-dogs had wallowed their beds in the snow and were silent. The moon was almost straight overhead, and a mile or two away a wolf pointed his muzzle to the radiant glow of it and howled. The sound, like a distant calling voice, added new fire to the growing thrill in Miki's blood. He turned in the direction of the wailing voice. He wanted to call back. He wanted to throw up his head and cry out to the forests, and the moon, and the starlit sky. But only his jaws clicked, and he looked at the tent in which Challoner was sleeping. He dropped down upon his belly in the snow. But his head was still alert and listening. The moon had already begun its westward decline. The fire burned out until the logs were only a dull and slumbering glow; the hand of Challoner's watch passed midnight, and still Miki was wide-eyed and restless in the thrill of the thing that was upon him. And then at last The Call that was coming to him from out of the night became his master, and he gnawed the babiche in two. It was the call of the Woman—of Nanette and the baby.

In his freedom Miki sniffed at the edge of Challoner's tent. His back sagged. His tail drooped. He knew that in this hour he was betraying the master for whom he had waited so long, and who had lived so vividly in his dreams. It was not reasoning, but an instinctive oppression of fact. He would come back. That conviction burned dully in his brain. But now—to-night—he must go. He slunk off into the darkness. With the stealth of a fox he made his way between the sleeping dogs. Not until he was a quarter of a mile from the camp did he straighten out, and then a gray and fleeting shadow he sped westward under the light of the moon.

There was no hesitation in the manner of his going. Free of the pain of his wounds, strong-limbed, deep-lunged as the strongest wolf of the forests, he went on tirelessly. Rabbits bobbing out of his path did not make him pause; even the strong scent of a fisher-cat almost under his nose did not swerve him a foot from his trail. Through swamp and deep forest, over lake and stream, across open barren and charred burns his unerring sense of orientation led him on. Once he stopped to drink where the swift current of a creek kept the water open. Even then he gulped in haste—and shot on. The moon drifted lower and lower until it sank into oblivion. The stars began to fade away The little ones went out, and the big ones grew sleepy and dull. A great snow-ghostly gloom settled over the forest world.

In the six hours between midnight and dawn he covered thirty-five miles.

And then he stopped. Dropping on his belly beside a rock at the crest of a ridge he watched the birth of day. With drooling jaws and panting breath he rested, until at last the dull gold of the winter sun began to paint the eastern sky. And then came the first bars of vivid sunlight, shooting over the eastern ramparts as guns flash from behind their battlements, and Miki rose to his feet and surveyed the morning wonder of his world. Behind him was Fort O' God, fifty miles away; ahead of him the cabin—twenty. It was the cabin he faced as he went down from the ridge.

As the miles between him and the cabin grew fewer and fewer he felt again something of the oppression that had borne upon him at Challoner's tent. And yet it was different. He had run his race. He had answered The Call. And now, at the end, he was seized by a fear of what his welcome would be. For at the cabin he had killed a man—and the man had belonged to the woman. His progress became more hesitating. Mid-forenoon found him only half a mile from the home of Nanette and the baby. His keen nostrils caught the faint tang of smoke in the air. He did not follow it up, but circled like a wolf, coming up stealthily and uncertainly until at last he looked out into the little clearing where a new world had come into existence for him. He saw the sapling cage in which Jacques Le Beau had kept him a prisoner; the door of that cage was still open, as Durant had left it after stealing him; he saw the ploughed-up snow where he had leapt upon the man-brute—and he whined.

He was facing the cabin door—and the door was wide open. He could see no life, but he could SMELL it. And smoke was rising from the chimney. He slunk across the open. In the manner of his going there was an abject humiliation—a plea for mercy if he had done wrong, a prayer to the creatures he worshipped that he might not be driven away.

He came to the door, and peered in. The room was empty. Nanette was not there. Then his ears shot forward and his body grew suddenly tense, and he listened, listened, LISTENED to a soft, cooing sound that was coming from the crib. He swallowed hard; the faintest whine rose in his throat and his claws CLICKED, CLICKED, CLICKED, across the floor and he thrust his great head over the side of the little bed. The baby was there. With his warm tongue he kissed it—just once—and then, with another deep breath, lay down on the floor.

He heard footsteps. Nanette came in with her arms filled with blankets; she carried these into the smaller room, and returned, before she saw him. For a moment she stared. Then, with a strange little cry, she ran to him; and once more he felt her arms about him; and he cried like a puppy with his muzzle against her breast, and Nanette laughed and sobbed, and in the crib the baby kicked and squealed and thrust her tiny moccasined feet up into the air.

"Ao-oo tap-wa-mukun" ("When the devil goes heaven comes in,") say the Crees. And with the death of Le Beau, her husband, the devil had gone out of life for Nanette. She was more beautiful than ever. Heaven was in the dark, pure glow of her eyes. She was no longer like a dog under the club and the whip of a brute, and in the re-birth of her soul she was glorious. Youth had come back to her—freed from the yoke of oppression. She was happy. Happy with her baby, with freedom, with the sun and the stars shining for her again; and with new

JAMES OLIVER CURWOOD

hope, the greatest star of all. Again on the night of that first day of his return Miki crept up to her when she was brushing her glorious hair. He loved to put his muzzle in it; he loved the sweet scent of it; he loved to put his head on her knees and feel it smothering him. And Nanette hugged him tight, even as she hugged the baby, for it was Miki who had brought her freedom, and hope, and life. What had passed was no longer a tragedy. It was justice. God had sent Miki to do for her what a father or a brother would have done.

And the second night after that, when Challoner came early in the darkness, it happened that Nanette had her hair down in that same way; and Challoner, seeing her thus, with the lampglow shining in her eyes, felt that the world had taken a sudden swift turn under his feet—that through all his years he had been working forward to this hour.

XXIII

With the coming of Challoner to the cabin of Nanette Le Beau there was no longer a shadow of gloom in the world for Miki. He did not reason out the wonder of it, nor did he have a foreboding for the future. It was the present in which he lived—the precious hours in which all the creatures he had ever loved were together. And yet, away back in his memory of those things that had grown deep in his soul, was the picture of Neewa, the bear; Neewa, his chum, his brother, his fighting comrade of many battles, and he thought of the cold and snow-smothered cavern at the top of the ridge in which Neewa had buried himself in that long and mysterious sleep that was so much like death. But it was in the present that he lived. The hours lengthened themselves out into days, and still Challoner did not go, nor did Nanette leave with the Indian for Fort O' God. The Indian returned with a note for MacDonnell in which Challoner told the Factor that something was the matter with the baby's lungs, and that she could not travel until the weather, which was intensely cold, grew warmer. He asked that the Indian be sent back with certain supplies.

In spite of the terrific cold which followed the birth of the new year Challoner had put up his tent in the edge of the timber a hundred yards from the cabin, and Miki divided his time between the cabin and the tent. For him they were glorious days. And for Challoner—

In a way Miki saw, though it was impossible for him to comprehend. As the days lengthened into a week, and the week into two, there was something in the glow of Nanette's eyes that had never been there before, and in the sweetness of her voice a new thrill, and in her prayers at night the thankfulness of a new and great joy.

And then, one day, Miki looked up from where he was lying beside the baby's crib and he saw Nanette in his master's arms, her face turned up to him, her eyes filled with the glory of the stars, and Challoner was saying something which transformed her face into the face of an angel. Miki was puzzled. And he was more puzzled when Challoner came from Nanette to the crib, and snuggled the baby up in his arms; and the woman—looking at them both for a moment with that wonderful look in her eyes—suddenly covered her face with her hands and sobbed. Half a snarl rose in Miki's throat, but in that moment Challoner had put his arm around Nanette too, and Nanette's arms were about him

JAMES OLIVER CURWOOD

and the baby, and she was sobbing something which for the life of him Miki could make neither head nor tail of. And yet he knew that he must not snarl or spring. He felt the wonder-thrill of the new thing that had come into the cabin; he gulped hard, and looked. A moment or two later Nanette was on her knees beside him, and her arms were around him, just as they had been around the man. And Challoner was dancing like a boy—cooing to the baby in his arms. Then he, too, dropped down beside Miki, and cried:

"My Gawd! Miki—I've Got A Fam'ly!"

And Miki tried to understand.

That night, after supper, he saw Challoner unbraid Nanette's glorious hair, and brush it. They laughed like two happy children. Miki tried still harder to understand.

When Challoner went to go to his tent in the edge of the forest he took Nanette in his arms, and kissed her, and stroked her shining hair; and Nanette took his face between her hands and smiled and almost cried in her joy.

After that Miki DID understand. He knew that happiness had come to all who were in that cabin.

Now that his world was settled, Miki took once more to hunting. The thrill of the trail came back to him, and wider and wider grew his range from the cabin. Again he followed Le Beau's old trapline. But the traps were sprung now. He had lost a great deal of his old caution. He had grown fatter. He no longer scented danger in every whiff of the wind. It was in the third week of Challoner's stay at the cabin, the day which marked the end of the cold spell and the beginning of warm weather, that Miki came upon an old dead-fall in a swamp a full ten miles from the clearing. Le Beau had set it for lynx, but nothing had touched the bait, which was a chunk of caribou flesh, frozen solid as a rock. Curiously Miki began smelling of it. He no longer feared danger. Menace had gone out of his world. He nibbled. He pulled— and the log crashed down to break his back. Only by a little did it fail. For twenty-four hours it held him helpless and crippled. Then, fighting through all those hours, he dragged himself out from under it. With the rising temperature a soft snow had fallen, covering all tracks and trails. Through this snow Miki dragged himself, leaving a path like that of an otter in the mud, for his hind quarters were helpless. His back was not broken; it was temporarily paralyzed by the blow and the weight of the log.

He made in the direction of the cabin, but every foot that he dragged himself was filled with agony, and his progress was so slow that at the end of an hour he had not gone more than a quarter of a mile. Another night found him less than two miles from the deadfall. He pulled himself under a shelter of brush and lay there until dawn. All through that day he did not move. The next, which was the fourth since he had left the cabin to hunt, the pain in his back was not so great. But he could pull himself through the snow only a few yards at a time. Again the good spirit of the forests favoured him for in the afternoon he came upon the partly eaten carcass of a buck killed by the wolves. The flesh was frozen but he gnawed at it ravenously. Then he found himself a shelter under a mass of fallen tree-tops, and for ten days thereafter he lay between life and death. He would have died had it not been for the buck. To the carcass he managed to drag himself, sometimes each day and sometimes every other day, and kept himself from starving. It was the end of the second week before he could stand well on his feet. The fifteenth day he returned to the cabin.

In the edge of the clearing there fell upon him slowly a foreboding of great change. The cabin was there. It was no different than it had been fifteen days ago. But out of the chimney there came no smoke, and the windows were white with frost. About it the snow lay clean and white, like an unspotted sheet. He made his way hesitatingly across the clearing to the door. There were no tracks. Drifted snow was piled high over the sill. He whined, and scratched at the door. There was no answer. And he heard no sound.

He went back into the edge of the timber, and waited. He waited all through that day, going occasionally to the cabin, and smelling about it, to convince himself that he had not made a mistake. When darkness came he hollowed himself out a bed in the fresh snow close to the door and lay there all through the night. Day came again, gray and empty and still there was no smoke from the chimney or sound from within the log walls, and at last he knew that Challoner and Nanette and the baby were gone. But he was hopeful. He no longer listened for sound from within the cabin, but watched and listened for them to come from out of the forest. He made short quests, hunting now on this side and now on that of the cabin, sniffing futilely at the fresh and trackless snow and pointing the wind for minutes at a time. In the afternoon, with a forlorn slouch to his body, he went deeper into the forest to hunt for a rabbit. When he had killed and eaten his supper he returned again and slept a second night in the burrow beside the door. A third day and a third night he remained, and the third night he heard the wolves howling under a clear and star-filled sky, and from him there came his first cry—a yearning, grief-filled cry that rose wailingly out of the clearing; the entreaty for his master, for Nanette, and the baby. It was not an answer to the wolves. In its note there was a trembling fear, the voicing of a thing that had grown into hopelessness.

And now there settled upon him a loneliness greater than any loneliness he had ever known. Something seemed to whisper to his canine brain that all he had seen and felt had been but a dream, and that he was face to face with his old world again, its dangers, its vast and soul-breaking emptiness, its friendlessness, its ceaseless strife for existence. His instincts, dulled by the worship of what the cabin had held, became keenly alive. He sensed again the sharp thrill of danger, which comes of ALONENESS, and his old caution fell upon him, so that the fourth day he slunk around the edge of the clearing like a wolf.

The fifth night he did not sleep in the clearing but found himself a windfall a mile back in the forest. That night he had strange and troubled dreams. They were not of Challoner, or of Nanette and the baby, nor were they of the fight and the unforgettable things he had seen at the Post. His dreams were of a high and barren ridge smothered in deep snow, and of a cavern that was dark and deep. Again he was with his brother and comrade of days that were gone—Neewa the bear. He was trying to waken him, and he could feel the warmth of his body and hear his sleepy, protesting grunts. And then, later, he was fighting again in the paradise of black currants, and with Neewa was running for his life from the enraged she-bear who had invaded their coulee. When he awoke suddenly from out of these dreams he was trembling and his muscles were tense. He growled in the darkness. His eyes were round balls of searching fire. He whined softly and yearningly in that pit of gloom under the windfall, and for a moment or two he listened, for he thought that Neewa might answer.

For a month after that night he remained near the cabin. At least once each day, and sometimes at night, he would return to the clearing. And more and more frequently he was thinking of Neewa. Early in March came the Tiki-Swao—(the Big Thaw). For a week the sun shone without a cloud in the sky. The air was warm. The snow turned soft underfoot and on the sunny sides of slopes and ridges it melted away into trickling streams or rolled down in "slides" that were miniature avalanches. The world was vibrant with a new thrill. It pulsed with the growing heart-beat of spring, and in Miki's soul there arose slowly a new hope, a new impression a new inspiration that was the thrilling urge of a wonderful instinct. NEEWA WOULD BE WAKING NOW!

It came to him at last like a voice which he could understand. The trickling music of the growing streams sang it to him; he heard it in the warm winds that were no longer filled with the blast of winter; he caught it in the new odours that were rising out of the earth; he smelled it in the dank, sweet perfume of the black woods-soil. The thing thrilled him. It called him. And he KNEW!

NEEWA WOULD BE WAKING NOW!

He responded to the call. It was in the nature of things that no power less than physical force could hold him back. And yet he did not travel as he had travelled from Challoner's camp to the cabin of Nanette and the baby. There had been a definite object there, something to achieve, something to spur him on to an immediate fulfilment. Now the thing that drew him, at first, was an overpowering impulse, not a reality. For two or three days his trail westward was wandering and indefinite. Then it straightened out, and early in the morning of the fifth day he came from a deep forest into a plain, and across that plain he saw the ridge. For a long time he gazed over the level space before he went on.

In his brain the pictures of Neewa were becoming clearer and clearer. After all, it seemed only yesterday or the day before that he had gone away from that ridge. Then it was smothered in snow, and a gray, terrible gloom had settled upon the earth. Now there was but little snow, and the sun was shining, and the sky was blue again. He went on, and sniffed along the foot of the ridge; he had not forgotten the way. He was not excited, because time had ceased to have definite import for him. Yesterday he had come down from that ridge, and to-day he was going back. He went straight to the mouth of Neewa's den, which was uncovered now, and thrust in his head and shoulders, and sniffed. Ah! but that lazy rascal of a bear was a sleepy-head! He was still sleeping. Miki could smell him. Listening hard, he could HEAR him.

He climbed over the low drift of snow that had packed itself in the neck of the cavern and entered confidently into the darkness. He heard a soft, sleepy grunt and a great sigh. He almost stumbled over Neewa, who had changed his bed. Again Neewa grunted, and Miki whined. He ran his muzzle into Neewa's fresh, new coat of spring fur and smelled his way to Neewa's ear. After all, it was only yesterday! And

　　　　　　　　　　　JAMES OLIVER CURWOOD

he remembered everything now! So he gave Neewa's ear a sudden sharp nip with his teeth, and then he barked in that low, throaty way that Neewa had always understood.

"Wake up, Neewa," it all said. "Wake up! The snow is gone, and it's fine out to-day. WAKE UP!"

And Neewa, stretching himself, gave a great yawn.

XXIV

Meshaba, the old Cree, sat on the sunny side of a rock on the sunny side of a slope that looked up and down the valley. Meshaba—who many, many years ago had been called The Giant—was very old. He was so old that even the Factor's books over at Fort O' God had no record of his birth; nor the "post logs" at Albany House, or Cumberland House, or Norway House, or Fort Churchill. Perhaps farther north, at Lac La Biche, at Old Fort Resolution, or at Fort McPherson some trace of him might have been found. His skin was crinkled and weather-worn, like dry buckskin, and over his brown, thin face his hair fell to his shoulders, snow-white. His hands were thin, even his nose was thin with the thinness of age. But his eyes were still like dark garnets, and down through the greater part of a century their vision had come undimmed.

They roved over the valley now. At Meshaba's back, a mile on the other side of the ridge, was the old trapper's cabin, where he lived alone. The winter had been long and cold, and in his gladness at the coming of spring Meshaba had come up the ridge to bask in the sun and look out over the changing world. For an hour his eyes had travelled up and down the valley like the eyes of an old and wary hawk. The dark spruce and cedar forest edged in the far side of the valley; between that and the ridge rolled the meadowy plain—still covered with melting snow in places, and in others bare and glowing, a dull green in the sunlight. From where he sat Meshaba could also see a rocky scarp of the ridge that projected out into the plain a hundred yards away. But this did not interest him, except that if it had not been in his line of vision he could have seen a mile farther down the valley.

In that hour of Sphinx-like watching, while the smoke curled slowly up from his black pipe, Meshaba had seen life. Half a mile from where he was sitting a band of caribou had come out of the timber and wandered into a less distant patch of low bush. They had not thrilled his old blood with the desire to kill, for there was already a fresh carcass hung up at the back of his cabin. Still farther away he had seen a hornless moose, so grotesque in its spring ugliness that the parchment-like skin of his face had cracked for half an instant in a smile, and out of him had come a low and appreciative grunt; for Meshaba, in spite of his age, still had a sense of humour left. Once he had seen a wolf, and twice a fox, and now his eyes were on an eagle high over his head. Meshaba would not have shot that eagle, for year after year it had come down through time with him, and it was always there soaring in the sun when spring came. So Meshaba grunted as he watched it, and was glad that Upisk had not died during the winter.

"Kata y ati sisew," he whispered to himself, a glow of superstition in his fiery eyes. "We have lived long together, and it is fated that we die together, Oh Upisk. The spring has come for us many times, and soon the black winter will swallow us up for ever."

His eyes shifted slowly, and then they rested on the scarp of the ridge that shut out his vision. His heart gave a sudden thump in his body. His pipe fell from his mouth to his hand; and he stared without moving, stared like a thing of rock.

On a flat sunlit shelf not more than eighty or ninety yards away stood a young black bear. In the warm glow of the sunlight the bear's spring coat shone like polished jet. But it was not the sudden appearance of the bear that amazed Meshaba. It was the fact that another animal was standing shoulder to shoulder with Wakayoo, and that it was not a brother bear, but a huge wolf. Slowly one of his thin hands rose to his eyes and he wiped away what he thought must surely be a strange something that was fooling his vision. In all his eighty years and odd he had never known a wolf to be thus friendly with a bear. Nature had made them enemies. Nature had fore-doomed their hatred to be the deepest hatred of the forests. Therefore, for a space, Meshaba doubted his eyes. But in another moment he saw that the miracle had truly come to pass. For the wolf turned broadside to him and it WAS a wolf! A huge, big-boned beast that stood as high at the shoulders as Wakayoo, the bear; a great beast, with a great head, and—

It was then that Meshaba's heart gave another thump, for the tail of a wolf is big and bushy in the springtime, and the tail of this beast was as bare of hair as a beaver's tail!

"Ohne moosh!" gasped Meshaba, under his breath—"a dog!"

He seemed to draw slowly into himself, slinking backward. His rifle stood just out of reach on the other side of the rock.

At the other end of that eighty or ninety yards Neewa and Miki stood blinking in the bright sunlight, with the mouth of the cavern in which Neewa had slept so many months just behind them. Miki was puzzled. Again it seemed to him that it was only yesterday, and not months ago, that he had left Neewa in that den, sleeping his lazy head off. And now that he had returned to him after his own hard winter in the forests he was astonished to find Neewa so big. For Neewa had grown steadily through his four months' nap and he was half again as big as when he went to sleep. Could Miki have spoken Cree, and had Meshaba given him the opportunity, he might have explained the situation.

"You see, Mr. Indian"—he might have said—"this dub of a bear and I have been pals from just about the time we were born. A man named Challoner tied us together first when Neewa, there, was just about as big as your head, and we did a lot of scrapping before we got properly acquainted. Then we got lost, and after that we hitched up like brothers; and we had a lot of fun and excitement all through last summer, until at last, when the cold weather came, Neewa hunted up this hole in the ground and the lazy cuss went to sleep for all winter. I won't mention what happened to me during the winter. It was a-plenty. So this spring I had a hunch it was about time for Neewa to get the cobwebs out of his fool head, and came back. And—here we are! But tell me this: WHAT MAKES NEEWA SO BIG?"

It was at least that thought—the bigness of Neewa—that was filling Miki's head at the present moment. And Meshaba, in place of listening to an explanation, was reaching for his rifle—while Neewa, with his brown muzzle sniffing the wind, was gathering in a strange smell. Of the three, Neewa saw nothing to be wondered at in the situation itself. When he had gone to sleep four and a half months ago Miki was at his side; and to-day, when he awoke, Miki was still at his side. The four and a half months meant nothing to him. Many times he and Miki had gone to sleep, and had awakened together. For all the knowledge he had of time it might have been only last night that he had fallen asleep.

The one thing that made Neewa uneasy now was that strange odour he had caught in the air. Instinctively he seized upon it as a menace—at least as something that he would rather NOT smell than smell. So he turned away with a warning WOOF to Miki. When Meshaba peered around the edge of the rock, expecting an easy shot, he caught only a flash of the two as they were disappearing. He fired quickly.

To Miki and Neewa the report of the rifle and the moaning whirr of the bullet over their backs recalled memories of a host of things, and Neewa settled down to that hump-backed, flat-eared flight of his that kept Miki pegging along at a brisk pace for at least a mile. Then Neewa stopped, puffing audibly. Inasmuch as he had had nothing to eat for a third of a year, and was weak from long inactivity, the run came within an ace of putting him out of business. It was several minutes before he could gather his wind sufficiently to grunt. Miki, meanwhile, was carefully smelling of him from his rump to his muzzle. There was apparently nothing missing, for he gave a delighted little yap at the end, and, in spite of his size and the dignity of increased age, he began frisking about Neewa In a manner emphatically expressive of his joy at his comrade's awakening.

"It's been a deuce of a lonely winter, Neewa, and I'm tickled to death to see you on your feet again," his antics said. "What'll we do? Go for a hunt?"

This seemed to be the thought in Neewa's mind, for he headed straight up the valley until they came to an open fen where he proceeded to quest about for a dinner of roots and grass; and as he searched he grunted—grunted in his old, companionable, cubbish way. And Miki, hunting with him, found that once more the loneliness had gone out of his world.

XXV

To Miki and Neewa, especially Neewa, there seemed nothing extraordinary in the fact that they were together again, and that their comradeship was resumed. Although during his months of hibernation Neewa's body had grown, his mind had not changed its memories or its pictures. It had not passed through a mess of stirring events such as had made the winter a thrilling one for Miki, and so it was Neewa who accepted the new situation most casually. He went on feeding as if nothing at all unusual had happened during the past four months, and after the edge had gone from his first hunger he fell into his old habit of looking to Miki for leadership. And Miki fell into the old ways as though only a day or a week and not four months had lapsed in their brotherhood. It is possible that he tried mightily to tell Neewa what had happened. At least he must have had that desire—to let him know in what a strange way he had found his old master, Challoner, and how he had lost him again. And also how he found the woman, Nanette, and the little baby Nanette, and how for a long time he had lived with them and loved them as he had never loved anything else on earth.

It was the old cabin, far to the north and east, that drew him now—the cabin in which Nanette and the baby had lived; and it was toward this cabin that he lured Neewa during the first two weeks of their hunting. They did not travel quickly, largely because of Neewa's voracious spring appetite and the fact that it consumed nine tenths of his waking hours to keep full on such provender as roots and swelling buds and grass. During the first week Miki grew either hopeless or disgusted in his hunting. One day he killed five rabbits and Neewa ate four of them and grunted piggishly for more.

If Miki had stood amazed and appalled at Neewa's appetite in the days of their cubhood and puppyhood a year ago, he was more than astounded now, for in the matter of food Neewa was a bottomless pit. On the other hand he was jollier than ever, and in their wrestling matches he was almost more than a match for Miki, being nearly again as heavy. He very soon acquired the habit of taking advantage of this superiority of weight, and at unexpected moments he would hop on Miki and pin him to the ground, his fat body smothering him like a huge soft cushion, and his arms holding him until at times Miki

JAMES OLIVER CURWOOD

could scarcely squirm. Now and then, hugging him in this embrace, he would roll over and over, both of them snarling and growling as though in deadly combat. This play, though he was literally the under dog, delighted Miki until one day they rolled over the edge of a deep ravine and crashed in a dog-and-bear avalanche to the bottom. After that, for a long time, Neewa did not roll with his victim. Whenever Miki wanted to end a bout, however, all he had to do was to give Neewa a sharp nip with his long fangs and the bear would uncoil himself and hop to his feet like a spring. He had a most serious respect for Miki's teeth.

But Miki's greatest moments of joy were where Neewa stood up man-fashion. Then was a real tussle. And his greatest hours of disgust were when Neewa stretched himself out in a tree for a nap.

It was the beginning of the third week before they came one day to the cabin. There was no change in it, and Miki's body sagged disconsolately as he and Neewa looked at it from the edge of the clearing. No smoke, no sign of life, and the window was broken now—probably by an inquisitive bear or a wolverine. Miki went to the window and stood up to it, sniffing inside. The SMELL was still there—so faint that he could only just detect it. But that was all. The big room was empty except for the stove, a table and a few bits of rude furniture. All else was gone. Three or four times during the next half hour Miki stood up at the window, and at last Neewa—urged by his curiosity—did likewise. He also detected the faint odour that was left in the cabin. He sniffed at it for a long time. It was like the smell he had caught the day he came out of his den—and yet different. It was fainter, more elusive, and not so unpleasant.

For a month thereafter Miki insisted on hunting in the vicinity of the cabin, held there by the "pull" of the thing which he could neither analyze nor quite understand. Neewa accepted the situation good-naturedly for a time. Then he lost patience and surrendered himself to a grouch for three whole days during which he wandered at his own sweet will. To preserve the alliance Miki was compelled to follow him. Berry time—early July—found them sixty miles north and west of the cabin, in the edge of the country where Neewa was born.

But there were few berries that summer of bebe nak um geda (the summer of drought and fire). As early as the middle of July a thin, gray film began to hover in palpitating waves over the forests. For three weeks there had been no rain. Even the nights were hot and dry. Each day the factors at their posts looked out with anxious eyes over their domains, and by the first of August every post had a score of halfbreeds and Indians patrolling the trails on the watch for fire. In their cabins and teepees the forest dwellers who had not gone to pass the summer at the posts waited and watched; each morning and noon and night they climbed tall trees and peered through that palpitating gray film for a sign of smoke. For weeks the wind came steadily from the south and west, parched as though swept over the burning sands of a desert. Berries dried up on the bushes; the fruit of the mountain ash shriveled on its stems; creeks ran dry; swamps turned into baked peat, and the poplar leaves hung wilted and lifeless, too limp to rustle in the breeze. Only once or twice in a lifetime does the forest dweller see poplar leaves curl up and die like that, baked to death in the summer sun. It is Kiskewahoon (the Danger Signal). Not only the warning of possible death in a holocaust of fire, but the omen of poor hunting and trapping in the winter to come.

Miki and Neewa were in a swamp country when the fifth of August came. In the lowland it was sweltering. Neewa's tongue hung from his mouth, and Miki was panting as they made their way along a black and sluggish stream that was like a great ditch and as dead as the day itself. There was no visible sun, but a red and lurid glow filled the sky— the sun struggling to fight its way through the smothering film that had grown thicker over the earth. Because they were in a "pocket"—a sweep of tangled country lower than the surrounding country— Neewa and Miki were not caught in this blackening cloud. Five miles away they might have heard the thunder of cloven hoofs and the crash of heavy bodies in their flight before the deadly menace of fire. As it was they made their way slowly through the parched swamp, so that it was midday when they came out of the edge of it and up through a green fringe of timber to the top of a ridge. Before this hour neither had passed through the horror of a forest fire. But it seized upon them now. It needed no past experience. The cumulative instinct of a thousand generations leapt through their brains and bodies. Their world was in the grip of Iskootao (the Fire Devil). To the south and the east and the west it was buried in a pall like the darkness of night, and out of the far edge of the swamp through which they had come they caught the first livid spurts of flame. From that direction, now that they were out of the "pocket," they felt a hot wind, and with that wind came a dull and rumbling roar that was like the distant moaning of a cataract. They waited, and watched, struggling to get their bearings, their minds fighting for a few moments in the gigantic process of changing instinct into reasoning and understanding. Neewa, being a bear, was afflicted with the near-sightedness of his breed, and he could see neither the black tornado of smoke bearing down upon them nor the flames leaping out of the swamp. But he could SMELL, and his nose was twisted into a hundred wrinkles, and even ahead of Miki he was ready for flight. But Miki, whose vision was like a hawk's, stood as if fascinated.

The roaring grew more distinct. It seemed on all sides of them. But it was from the south that there came the first storm of ash rushing noiselessly ahead of the fire, and after that the smoke. It was then that Miki turned with a strange whine but it was Neewa now who took the lead—Neewa, whose forebears had ten thousand times run this same wild race with death in the centuries since their world was born. He did not need the keenness of far vision now. He KNEW. He knew what was behind, and what was on either side, and where the one trail to safety lay; and in the air he felt and smelled the thing that was death. Twice Miki made efforts to swing their course into the east, but Neewa would have none of it. With flattened ears he went on NORTH. Three times Miki stopped to turn and face the galloping menace behind them, but never for an instant did Neewa pause. Straight on—NORTH, NORTH, NORTH—north to the higher lands, the big waters, the open plains.

They were not alone. A caribou sped past them with the swiftness of the wind itself. "FAST, FAST, FAST!"—Neewa's instinct cried; "but—ENDURE! For the caribou, speeding even faster than the fire, will fall of exhaustion shortly and be eaten up by the flames. FAST—but ENDURE!"

And steadily, stoically, at his loping gait Neewa led on.

A bull moose swung half across their trail from the west, wind-gone and panting as though his throat were cut. He was badly burned, and running blindly into the eastern wall of fire.

Behind and on either side, where the flames were rushing on with the pitiless ferocity of hunnish regiments, the harvest of death was a vast and shuddering reality. In hollow logs, under windfalls, in the thick tree-tops, and in the earth itself, the smaller things of the wilderness sought their refuge—and died. Rabbits became leaping balls of flame, then lay shrivelled and black; the marten were baked in their trees; fishers and mink and ermine crawled into the deepest corners of the windfalls and died there by inches; owls fluttered out of their tree-tops, staggered for a few moments in the fiery air, and fell down into the heart of the flame. No creature made a sound—except the porcupines; and as they died they cried like little children.

In the green spruce and cedar timber, heavy with the pitch that made their thick tops spurt into flame like a sea of explosive, the fire rushed on with a tremendous roar. From it—in a straight race—there was no escape for man or beast. Out of that world of conflagration there might have risen one great, yearning cry to heaven: WATER—WATER—WATER! Wherever there was water there was also hope—and life. Breed and blood and wilderness feuds were forgotten in the great hour of peril. Every lake became a haven of refuge.

To such a lake came Neewa, guided by an unerring instinct and sense of smell sharpened by the rumble and roar of the storm of fire behind him. Miki had "lost" himself; his senses were dulled; his nostrils caught no scent but that of a world in flames—so, blindly, he followed his comrade. The fire was enveloping the lake along its western shore, and its water was already thickly tenanted. It was not a large lake, and almost round. Its diameter was not more than two hundred yards. Farther out—a few of them swimming, but most of them standing on bottom with only their heads out of water—were a score of caribou and moose. Many other shorter-legged creatures were swimming aimlessly, turning this way and that, paddling their feet only enough to keep afloat. On the shore where Neewa and Miki paused was a huge porcupine, chattering and chuckling foolishly, as if scolding all things in general for having disturbed him at dinner. Then he took to the water. A little farther up the shore a fisher-cat and a fox hugged close to the water line, hesitating to wet their precious fur until death itself snapped at their heels; and as if to bring fresh news of this death a second fox dragged himself wearily out on the shore, as limp as a wet rag after his swim from the opposite shore, where the fire was already leaping in a wall of flame. And as this fox swam in, hoping to find safety, an old bear twice as big as Neewa, crashed panting from the undergrowth, plunged into the water, and swam OUT. Smaller things were creeping and crawling and slinking along the shore; little red-eyed ermine, marten, and mink, rabbits, squirrels, and squeaking gophers, and a horde of mice. And at last, with these things which he would have devoured so greedily running about him, Neewa waded slowly out into the water. Miki followed until he was submerged to his shoulders. Then he stopped. The fire was close now,

JAMES OLIVER CURWOOD

advancing like a race-horse. Over the protecting barrier of thick timber drove the clouds of smoke and ash. Swiftly the lake became obliterated, and now out of that awful chaos of blackness and smoke and heat there rose strange and thrilling cries; the bleating of a moose calf that was doomed to die and the bellowing, terror-filled response of its mother; the agonized howling of a wolf; the terrified barking of a fox, and over all else the horrible screaming of a pair of loons whose home had been transformed into a sea of flame.

Through the thickening smoke and increasing heat Neewa gave his call to Miki as he began to swim, and with an answering whine Miki plunged after him, swimming so close to his big black brother that his muzzle touched the other's flank. In mid-lake Neewa did as the other swimming creatures were doing—paddled only enough to keep himself afloat; but for Miki, big of bone and unassisted by a life-preserver of fat, the struggle was not so easy. He was forced to swim to keep afloat. A dozen times he circled around Neewa, and then, with something of the situation driven upon him, he came up close to the bear and rested his forepaws on his shoulders.

The lake was now encircled by a solid wall of fire. Blasts of flame shot up the pitch-laden trees and leapt for fifty feet into the blistering air. The roar of the conflagration was deafening. It drowned all sound that brute agony and death may have made. And its heat was terrific. For a few terrible minutes the air which Miki drew into his lungs was like fire itself. Neewa plunged his head under water every few seconds, but it was not Miki's instinct to do this. Like the wolf and the fox and the fisher-cat and the lynx it was his nature to die before completely submerging himself.

Swift as it had come the fire passed; and the walls of timber that had been green a few moments before were black and shrivelled and dead; and sound swept on with the flame until it became once more only a low and rumbling murmur.

To the black and smouldering shores the live things slowly made their way. Of all the creatures that had taken refuge in the lake many had died. Chief of those were the porcupines. All had drowned.

Close to the shore the heat was still intense, and for hours the earth was hot with smouldering fire. All the rest of that day and the night that followed no living thing moved out of the shallow water. And yet no living thing thought to prey upon its neighbour. The great peril had made of all beasts kin.

A little before dawn of the day following the fire relief came. A deluge of rain fell, and when day broke and the sun shone through a murky heaven there was left no sign of what the lake had been, except for the dead bodies that floated on its surface or lined its shores. The living things had returned into their desolated wilderness—and among them Neewa and Miki.

XXVI

For many days after the Great Fire it was Neewa who took the lead. All their world was a black and lifeless desolation and Miki would not have known which way to turn. Had it been a local fire of small extent he would have "wandered" out of its charred path. But the conflagration had been immense. It had swept over a vast reach of country, and for a half of the creatures who had saved themselves in the lakes and streams there was only a death by starvation left.

But not for Neewa and his breed. Just as there had been no indecision in the manner and direction of his flight before the fire so there was now no hesitation in the direction he chose to seek a live world again. It was due north and west—as straight as a die. If they came to a lake, and went around it, Neewa would always follow the shore until he came directly opposite his trail on the other side of the lake—and then strike north and west again. He travelled steadily, not only by day but also by night, with only short intervals of rest, and the dawning of the second morning found Miki more exhausted than the bear.

There were many evidences now that they had reached a point where the fire had begun to burn itself out. Patches of green timber were left standing, there were swamps unscathed by the flames, and here and there they came upon green patches of meadow. In the swamps and timber they feasted, for these oases in what had been a sea of flame were filled with food ready to be preyed upon and devoured. For the first time Neewa refused to stop because there was plenty to eat. The sixth day they were a hundred miles from the lake in which they had sought refuge from the fire.

It was a wonderful country of green timber, of wide plains and of many lakes and streams—cut up by a thousand usayow (low ridges), which made the best of hunting. Because it was a country of many waters, with live streams running between the ridges and from lake to lake, it had not suffered from the drought like the country farther south. For a month Neewa and Miki hunted in their new paradise, and became fat and happy again.

It was in September that they came upon a strange thing in the edge of a swamp. At first Miki thought that it was a cabin; but it was a great deal smaller than any cabin he had known. It was not much larger than the cage of saplings in which Le Beau had kept him. But it was made of heavy logs, and the logs were notched so that nothing could knock them down. And these logs, instead of lying closely one on the other, had open spaces six or eight inches wide between them. And there was a wide-open door. From this strange contraption there came a strong odour of over-ripened fish. The smell repelled Miki. But it was a powerful attraction to Neewa, who persisted in remaining near it in spite of all Miki could do to drag him away. Finally, disgusted at his comrade's bad taste, Miki sulked off alone to hunt. It was some time after that before Neewa dared to thrust his head and shoulders through the opening. The smell of the fish made his little eyes gleam. Cautiously he stepped inside the queer looking thing of logs. Nothing happened. He saw the fish, all he could eat, just on the other side of a sapling against which he must lean to reach them. He went deliberately to the sapling, leaned over, and then!—

"CRASH!"

He whirled about as if shot. There was no longer an opening where he had entered. The sapling "trigger" had released an over-head door, and Neewa was a prisoner. He was not excited, but accepted the situation quite coolly, probably having no doubt in his mind that somewhere there was an aperture between the logs large enough for him to squeeze through. After a few inquisitive sniffs he proceeded to devour the fish. He was absorbed in his odoriferous feast when out of a clump of dwarf balsams a few yards away appeared an Indian. He quickly took in the situation, turned, and disappeared.

Half an hour later this Indian ran into a clearing in which were the recently constructed buildings of a new Post. He made for the Company store. In the fur-carpeted "office" of this store a man was bending fondly over a woman. The Indian saw them as he entered, and chuckled. "Sakehewawin" ("the love couple"); that was what they had already come to call them at Post Lac Bain—this man and woman who had given them a great feast when the missioner had married them not so very long ago. The man and the woman stood up when the Indian entered, and the woman smiled at him. She was beautiful. Her eyes were glowing, and there was the flush of a flower in her cheeks. The Indian felt the worship of her warm in his heart.

"Oo-ee, we have caught the bear," he said. "But it is napao (a he-bear). There is no cub, Iskwao Nanette!"

The white man chuckled.

"Aren't we having the darndest luck getting you a cub for a house-pet,

JAMES OLIVER CURWOOD

Nanette?" he asked. "I'd have sworn this mother and her cub would have been easily caught. A he-bear! We'll have to let him loose, Mootag. His pelt is good for nothing. Do you want to go with us and see the fun, Nanette?"

She nodded, her little laugh filled with the joy of love and life.

"Oui. It will be such fun—to see him go!"

Challoner led the way, with an axe in his hand; and with him came Nanette, her hand in his. Mootag followed with his rifle, prepared for an emergency. From the thick screen of balsams Challoner peered forth, then made a hole through which Nanette might look at the cage and its prisoner. For a moment or two she held her breath as she watched Neewa pacing back and forth, very much excited now. Then she gave a little cry, and Challoner felt her fingers pinch his own sharply. Before he knew what she was about to do she had thrust herself through the screen of balsams.

Close to the log prison, faithful to his comrade in the hour of peril, lay Miki. He was exhausted from digging at the earth under the lower log, and he had not smelled or heard anything of the presence of others until he saw Nanette standing not twenty paces away. His heart leapt up into his panting throat. He swallowed, as though to get rid of a great lump; he stared. And then, with a sudden, yearning whine, he sprang toward her. With a yell Challoner leapt out of the balsams with uplifted axe. But before the axe could fall, Miki was in Nanette's arms, and Challoner dropped his weapon with a gasp of amazement—and one word:

"Miki!"

Mootag, looking on in stupid astonishment, saw both the man and the woman making a great fuss over a strange and wild-looking beast that looked as if it ought to be killed. They had forgotten the bear. And Miki, wildly joyous at finding his beloved master and mistress, had forgotten him also. It was a prodigious Whoof from Neewa himself that brought their attention to him. Like a flash Miki was back at the pen smelling of Neewa's snout between two of the logs, and with a great wagging of tail trying to make him understand what had happened.

Slowly, with a thought born in his head that made him oblivious of all else but the big black brute in the pen, Challoner approached the trap. Was it possible that Miki could have made friends with any other bear than the cub of long ago? He drew in a deep breath as he looked at them. Neewa's brown-tipped nose was thrust between two of the logs and Miki Was Licking It With His Tongue! He held out a hand to Nanette, and when she came to him he pointed for a space, without speaking.

Then he said:

"It is the cub, Nanette. You know—the cub I have told you about. They've stuck together all this time—ever since I killed the cub's mother a year and a half ago, and tied them together on a piece of rope. I understand now why Miki ran away from us when we were at the cabin. He went back—to the bear."

To-day if you strike northward from Le Pas and put your canoe in the Rat River or Grassberry waterways, and thence paddle and run with the current down the Reindeer River and along the east shore of Reindeer Lake you will ultimately come to the Cochrane—and Post Lac Bain. It is one of the most wonderful countries in all the northland. Three hundred Indians, breeds and French, come with their furs to Lac Bain. Not a soul among them—man, woman, or child—but knows the story of the "tame bear of Lac Bain"—the pet of l'ange, the white angel, the Factor's wife.

The bear wears a shining collar and roams at will in the company of a great dog, but, having grown huge and fat now, never wanders far from the Post. And it is an unwritten law in all that country that the animal must not be harmed, and that no bear traps shall be set within five miles of the Company buildings. Beyond that limit the bear never roams; and when it comes cold, and he goes into his long sleep, he crawls into a deep warm cavern that has been dug for him under the Company storehouse. And with him, when the nights come, sleeps Miki the dog.

The End

JAMES OLIVER CURWOOD

A Note About the Author

James Oliver Curwood (1878–1927) was an American writer and conservationist popular in the action-adventure genre. Curwood began his career as a journalist, and was hired by the Canadian government to travel around Northern Canada and publish travel journals in order to encourage tourism. This served as a catalyst for his works of fiction, which were often set in Alaska or the Hudson Bay area in Canada. Curwood was among the top ten best-selling authors in the United States during the early and mid 1920s. Over one-hundred and eighty films have been inspired by or based on his work. With these deals paired with his record book sales, Curwood earned an impressive amount of wealth from his work. As he grew older, Curwood became an advocate for conservationism and environmentalism, giving up his hunting hobby and serving on conservation committees. Between his activism and his literary work, Curwood helped shape the popular perception of the natural world.

A Note from the Publisher

Spanning many genres, from non-fiction essays to literature classics to children's books and lyric poetry, Mint Edition books showcase the master works of our time in a modern new package. The text is freshly typeset, is clean and easy to read, and features a new note about the author in each volume. Many books also include exclusive new introductory material. Every book boasts a striking new cover, which makes it as appropriate for collecting as it is for gift giving. Mint Edition books are only printed when a reader orders them, so natural resources are not wasted. We're proud that our books are never manufactured in excess and exist only in the exact quantity they need to be read and enjoyed.

Discover more of your favorite classics with Bookfinity™.

- Track your reading with custom book lists.
- Get great book recommendations for your personalized Reader Type.
- Add reviews for your favorite books.
- AND MUCH MORE!

Visit **bookfinity.com** and take the fun Reader Type quiz to get started.

Enjoy our classic and modern companion pairings!